BUSHWHACKED!

Black Pete Bowen could handle just about anything, but when he was shot from his saddle and relieved of $2,000 and his horse by three hillbilly bandits, the young Reb saw red. Determined to seek revenge and restitution, Pete oiled his Smith and Wessons and set off after the villainous three. Meanwhile the bushwhackers had got themselves appointed as guides to beautiful Princess Sophie and her brother, but with robbery and murder in their hearts. Could Pete rescue the princess and overcome the fearsome odds against him. Slim chance! was so the belief these questions were answered.

Bl... ...t
an... ...s
sa... ...s
h... ...g
Re... ...e
an... ...d
W... ...s
th... ...d
go... ...o
be... ...,
bu... ...r
hearts. Could Pete rescue the princess and overcome the fearsome odds against him? Much lead was to fly before these questions were answered.

BUSHWHACKED!

Bushwhacked!

by
John Dyson

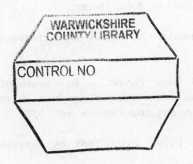
Dales Large Print Books
Long Preston, North Yorkshire,
England.

British Library Cataloguing in Publication Data.

Dyson, John
  Bushwhacked!

  A catalogue record for this book is
  available from the British Library

  ISBN 1-85389-890-2 pbk

First published in Great Britain by Robert Hale Ltd., 1997

Copyright © 1997 by John Dyson

Cover illustration © FABA by arrangement with Norma
Editorial

The right of John Dyson to be identified as the author of
this work has been asserted by him in accordance with the
Copyright, Designs and Patents Act, 1988

Published in Large Print 1998 by arrangement with Robert
Hale Ltd.

Dales Large Print is an imprint of
Library Magna Books Ltd.
Printed and bound in Great Britain by
T.J. International Ltd., Cornwall, PL28 8RW.

One

The lone rider came out of the vast oceanic emptiness of the great plains. Before him gradually rose the granite ramparts that signified the western frontier of the Indian Nations. After weeks of travelling halfway across the continent he felt like a sailor sighting land and knowing that his navigation had been sound. As he approached he could see more clearly two clear-cut peaks which he recognized as guardians of a crack in the cliffs known as Burford Gap. Through this steep defile he could climb to a different land, a place of hills and lakes and lush, game-filled valleys, a territory patrolled by the US Army from its forts, the beginning of 'civilization'.

'We've made it,' he said to his two

horses. 'We're half-way home. It'll be easy-ridin' now.'

The grey mare he was using as pack-horse on a loose leading rein to give her a rest blew out her cheeks with a splutter of agreement as if she understood his words. They had been together a long time. The sturdy-shouldered, paint-patch quarter horse he rode pricked her ears forward as he adjusted their direction to aim at the crevice in the hills.

'What's the matter, gal?' It was as if she had sensed something, someone, some creature up ahead. She was a younger, fatter filly than the mare, but had proved herself an able companion to the grey during the thousand-mile journey behind them. 'Maybe, when we git to Texas I'll put you both to stallion. Howja like that, gals?'

The rider was tall and straight-backed, young, only some twenty-one years, but his face was hardened by sun, weather and often-bitter experience. His faded and bullet-holed topcoat of Confederate grey told that he had been through the war, and his gaunt, black-bearded jaws had a grim set to them. His dark eyes peered from beneath his straight-brimmed hat at the line of hills. He had a sensation that all was not as hunky-dory as he had hoped. A sixth sense, a chill up his spine, warned him of danger. But he could see nothing amiss and he kneed the quarter-horse on.

'Maybe we're imagining things,' he muttered, sniffing at the air with his sharp nostrils.

They trailed on across the trackless buffalo grass towards the blue hills and he began to sing, as was his wont:

'I'm Captain Jinks of the Horse Marines,
'I feed my horse on corn and beans,
'And I often go beyond my means,
'I'm captain in the army ...'

The old Civil War ditty died on his lips and his mouth went dry as he suddenly discerned what had excited his horse. A line of Indians trickled out of the mouth of Burford Gap on their ponies. The line divided into two pincers and stood awaiting him. Comanches!

'Hot damn!' the Texan hissed through his teeth as he brought his horses to a halt and reached down to draw the 15–shot Winchester repeater from the boot. To turn tail and retreat into the emptiness of the plains would be futile. Nor, if he went south, down the Texan Panhandle and across Old Greer County, would he have much chance of throwing them off. More likely to run into more of their kind. This was their country out here beyond the line of forts.

They were still half a mile away. Comanche, sure enough. As dark as the Apache, almost burned black by the sun, and as wild and savage-looking. Some were half-naked, their legs and bodies bare, streaked with paint. Scalps or feathers were ruffled by the prairie wind at the sharp tips of their long lances. Others were in buckskins or captured army monkey-jackets, and a variety of headgear. Some wore feathers, others straw pill-boxes or beribboned plug hats. They had been raiding, sure enough. The Texan drew a thin brass telescope and saw that one in the centre, who appeared to be the leader, had his hair drawn up on top, caked with clay, in which was held a large painted bone.

'Red Bone,' he whispered. 'Is that butcher still about?'

He counted forty of them, waiting for him, taunting him. They knew they were between him and where he wanted to go. One consolation was only two or three appeared to have rifles in their hands, and those of the old-fashioned, muzzle-loading kind. But Comanche could be as deadly with arrow, lance and tomahawk as with bullets. If not more so.

'Waal, it sure ain't no use tryin' to parley. Not with Red Bone. I knew him before the war when I was a kid of fourteen and rode with the Rangers. He was always partial to burnin', torturin' and killin'. Guess I'd better present my compliments.'

The Texan levered the Winchester '66 and pumped a slug from the tubular spring-activated magazine beneath the barrel into the chamber—a .44 rimfire cartridge with 28 grains of black powder stopping power. The latest state of the art of rifle manufacture. He squinted along the sights and lined up on one of the riflemen. 'Iffen I take out the artillery we might be more fair-matched,' he muttered, fingering the trigger. He braced himself in the bentwood stirrups. 'Steady there, gal.'

He was used to explaining his moves to the horses, not having anyone else to talk to in the wilderness. Of course, he could have put a slug in each of them and used them as a barricade, but he was loath to do that. And the Comanche would have played a waiting game until his ammunition had gone. There was no other cover around on the bare plain. The only thing to do was take the fight to the enemy and hope against hope they didn't capture him alive.

'Now,' he whispered, and squeezed hard. Through the recoil, the explosion, the puff of black smoke, he saw, split-seconds later, one of the Indian riflemen throw up his arms and slide from his pony. He heard the angry howl from the line of Comanches as his startled paint shied beneath him. He repumped the lever, ejecting the spent shell as the horde of Indians charged towards him. 'Or never!' He took out a second of those brandishing a rifle, as a ball from another whistled past his own head.

'Stand hard, gals,' he yelled. 'I jest got one more to put down. And maybe that should be Red Bone.'

He found that talking to himself, or the horses, quelled the panic in him, helped him to concentrate. And what man would not have had panic rising in his gorge faced by a screaming mob of blood-thirsty

Comanche thundering towards him in their dust cloud? The Texan could discern their leader among them as they charged nearer and nearer across the flat ground. He gritted his teeth and fired a third time. But the paint snorted and flailed her hooves in fear of the oncoming tide and the bullet went wide.

'Come on,' he said, gripping the reins in his teeth, and touching spurs to her sides. 'Charge!'

He raced towards the line of Comanches, the grey pounding along behind, firing from the shoulder, three, four, five went down, before he hit them head on, and burst through them, brushing shoulders with warriors, as arrows zipped about him, and a lance cut through the cloth of his coat.

A shaven-headed Comanche leapt at him as they passed, trying to drag him from his horse. The Texan hammered the butt of the rifle into his face, knocking him clear. Glancing back he saw another warrior was astride the grey, reaching to fit an arrow into his bow. He fired the rifle from the hip, blasting him into Eternity, or wherever he might go.

He cantered away in a semi-circle, levering Oliver Winchester's life-saver, pursued by the band. *Ker-pow!* The former Johnny Reb inflicted more damage on them. If it was a fight they wanted they could have it. His dander was up and he was in a killing mood. He was thankful he was on the quarter horse. It had a high-powered momentum more than a match for the Comanches' scrubby, if spirited ponies, and went like a rocket over a quarter-mile, hence its name. The riderless grey was dragged along in their wake, coffee-pot and frying-pan jangling. In the tarpaulin-covered baggage roll was $3,000 in gold dust, coin and greenbacks, the profits of a year spent marshaling and bounty-hunting in Nevada.

The prospect of losing his hard-earned grubstake, the cash he planned to put down on a ranch in Texas, made the rider even more determined to fight. He rode around the desperate horde pounding his rifle at them mercilessly.

He heard a Comanche screaming his fate cry and out of the corner of his eye saw Red Bone riding at him from an oblique angle, coming at him, swinging a tomahawk. He ducked and felt the sharp flint whistle past his ear. He whirled the quarter horse about, levered and aimed at Red Bone's chest. There was an ominous click. His fifteen slugs were spent.

Red Bone howled his anger and slashed his tomahawk again. The Texan parried the blow with the rifle. They were up close, hammering at each other. For moments their dark eyes met and it was as if they recognized each other from the old days. With all his strength the Texan clouted the Comanche chief across the head with the heavy rifle, making him lose his grip on his pony and tumble, humiliatingly, into the grass.

The Texan viciously rowelled the paint,

expecting any second an arrow in his back, and set off across the plain for the gap in the hills. He could hear the grey galloping valiantly along behind. Not having a man to carry she could keep up.

He looked back, hanging low over the paint's neck, and saw Red Bone standing in the grass, cursing and waving his fist, as his warriors took up the pursuit. But they were putting distance between them and were out of range of their bows.

When they reached the narrow entry to Burford Gap the Texan scrambled to the ground, pulling the horses into the cover of some large rocks. He unbuttoned his grey coat and drew the twin pearl-handled Smith and Wesson .32s from his hip holsters. He used the cross-handed draw in which he was expert, and knelt to meet the onslaught. He cracked off several shots at the oncoming Comanche but they were having second thoughts. They had expected to have an easy cat-and-mouse game, not come up against a hardened, fast-shooting prairie rat. They took cover in the grass and made him keep his head down with the sibilant hiss of their arrows. They knew it would be suicide to charge.

Red Bone had caught his pony and came jogging up. The Texan sent a slug his way creasing his neck, and he spun his mount around, stopping it in its tracks. He slowly ambled the pony away, reconsidering his position. He had already lost thirteen of his men, killed and wounded by this one white man. How many shooting irons did he have? How much ammunition? He might lose another thirteen warriors by the time they had smoked him out.

'Who are you?' Red Bone shouted out in his own tongue.

The Texan grinned to himself He knew some Comanche lingo. 'Black Pit,' he yelled out, using the name his Cherokee brigade had given him during the war.

'Black Pit, you can go.' Chastened by the Texan's fire power, Red Bone was salvaging his pride. 'We will meet again.'

'I'm ready any time you are, Red Bone. I sure didn't start this. Take your injured an' go. You thought you could take my scalp, but it ain't your lucky day.'

'Today the gods smile on you. Another day will be different.'

'Maybe.' The Texan was carefully re-stocking the rifle magazine with bullets from his belt and muttered, 'Git outa here 'fore I put a slug in your guts, you lousy redskin.'

He gave a whistle of relief as he saw them go trailing away over the plain. 'Jeez, I weren't expecting to be still in the land of the living. Guess I am a lucky son-of-a-gun. Damn fool, Comanch'. If they had any sense they would have speared you damn horses, shot you out under me. But they never did have much sense.'

He took a swig from his water canteen, let the horses muzzle some from his palm. 'I told you we was nearly home.' He reholstered his revolvers, took the reins and led them on foot up the narrow ravine, scrambling up the precipitous ascent until he reached the clifftop some 500 feet above. He looked back across the sea of grass but it was devoid of humans. Red Bone and his band had disappeared into its emptiness.

'We're back in the Nations,' he said. 'We might make the Lac Qui Parle by sunset. It's a bit of a spooky sort of place to camp out, but if ghosts is all we got to worry about that's OK.'

He swung up on to the paint's back. It was a strange sensation being back in the Nations. He had spent three years here as officer in charge of the Cherokee Mounted Infantry. Once the Confederate flag had flown here. They had had their moments of glory, winning the day at Pea Ridge, only to lose it the next. After Fort Smith was lost and the Battle of Honey Springs, they had done most of their fighting retreating, a bitter succession of guerrilla attacks, blowing bridges, attacking forts and Union outposts, until they were forced further and further back across Indian Territory. Finally, months after Lee's surrender, when the half-caste Indian General Stand Watie had given up the fight, the Texan had disbanded the brigade, sent his boys back to their farms and villages to try to pick up the pieces. He, himself, had headed for Virginia City[1] to seek his fortune among the gold-miners. Yes, it was strange indeed to be back in this land. He planned to ride on through, cross the Red River and on down the trail to San Antonio. If he avoided the army patrols he shouldn't have any trouble.

The set-to with the Comanche had made him edgy. It seemed like a bad omen. And, although it was good to see the panorama of hills and streams again, being back in this country brought a nasty taste of defeat to his throat. 'All we gotta do is stay outa trouble,' he told the broncs. 'Thassall. An'

---

[1] See *Lousy Reb*

we'll be back home in no time.'

To cast away his doubts he re-started singing as he jogged along.

'I feed my broncs on corn and beans ...'

Two

The coloured Union soldiers of the Tenth Cavalry manning the newly built Fort Sill in the heart of Indian Territory grinned widely as four covered wagons trundled through the gates with its over-hanging blockhouse. They were used to missionaries, scouts, traders, hunters, homesteaders and tame feathered Indians coming and going but the folk on these wagons were a different kettle of fish. They were strangely garbed and gabbling in a tongue they were told was Russian. On the box of the leading wagon sat an effete little man with a goatee beard, resplendent in a white, bemedalled uniform and peaked cap. Beside him was a beautiful blonde girl, her dress of green taffeta, and her cloak trimmed with beaver.

The commander of the fort, Captain Franklin Hazeltin, came from his office to greet them and put out a hand to help the girl down. As he gazed into her blue eyes he went quite weak at the knees. 'May I enquire the nature of your journey, miss?' he asked.

'Have you not been informed by your government?' Her tiny hand clung on to his own. 'This is my brother, Count Alexis, cousin of the Grand Duke of Vladimir and, as such, related to the Tsar.'

The dapper little guy jumped down, clicked his heels and offered a soft and moist hand. 'Ve vere told zat every courtesy vould be at our disposal. Zis is my sister, ze Princess Sophie. Ve are very veery from our journey. Perhaps you show us to our quarters?'

'I'm sorry. This is something of a surprise. I have had no news of your arrival. We're very cut off from things here,' Hazeltin protested, somewhat flustered by the royal arrivals.

'No matter,' the princess replied. 'No need to make a fuss. If you have a spare cabin, I have my maid'—she indicated a dumpy young woman dressed in black who tumbled from the back of the wagon. She was hanging on to a large white poodle dog—'and my servants.' Men with beards were climbing from the other wagons, bustling about, shouting to each other in their odd lingo. 'We have brought our own beds. As long as you have somewhere for my brother and I, for my maid and butler, anywhere will do for the rest.'

'But ... er ... milady,' Hazeltin stuttered, extricating his fingers from hers. 'What are you doing here?'

'Doing?' the count expostulated in his peculiar accent. 'Ve are leading ze hunting party. Ze first royal Russian hunting party into ze wilderness of ze American Vest.'

'Your President, himself, when we called on him at the White House suggested we came to see Indian Territory,' the princess put in.

'Zat is so. At ze Vite House,' the count said. 'A charming man.'

'Oh, I see,' Captain Hazeltin replied. 'Yes, of course. I will do everything in my power to make your trip a success. There is a cabin a couple of my lieutenants are sharing. I'm sure they won't mind moving out.'

'Excuse, pliz,' the count said. 'Zese soldiers here, zey are all blacks?'

'Yes, this is an all-black regiment, except for me, of course.'

'But I thought ze blacks is ze slaves.'

'No, that's all changed now, since the war,' Captain Hazeltin smiled. 'That's what it was all about.'

'Really?' Princess Sophie cooed. 'How sweet.'

'If you care to come into my office I will have your chamber, I mean cabin, prepared. And I hope you will honour us with your presence at dinner in the officers' mess?'

'Certainly,' Sophie trilled, and tucked

her arm into the captain's own. 'We have brought all kind of goodies along. We would like to contribute. Do you love champagne and caviar? It keeps Alexis from being homesick. This is his first time away from Russia.'

'You speak excellent English, yourself, Princess.'

'Of course, I was tutored in Berlin and Paris, and finished in London. This is my first time in America.'

'May I hope your first time is most enjoyable,' Captain Hazeltin said and, for some reason, blushed scarlet as he stared at her.

He was not an unhandsome young man, fresh out on the frontier from West Point, and sported a goatee-like beard, himself, but black and bushy, unlike the count's little vee. He came from a good Boston family who had hoped for a better posting for their youngest son than this far-flung outpost.

He seated them in his office, instructed

his sergeant to offer them coffee, and took his leave. 'I will go see to your accommodations, your ... your ... count and princess.'

As he closed the door he had an odd sensation that he heard them burst into laughter.

'I will have your certificate of permission to hunt signed for you in the morning, Count,' Captain Hazeltin said as he welcomed his Russian guests to the officers' mess. 'There is usually a fee of fifty dollars but we will, of course, waive that in your honour.'

He felt sure he was doing the right thing. If they were personal friends of President Ulysses Grant he would have to pull out all stops for them. Grant might be a lousy president but he had been a great war leader. Hazeltin stroked aside his thick locks of long black hair that had the habit of swinging across his brow. He was in his best uniform, as were his officers. He was not sure he shouldn't have given up his place at the head of the table to the count—he was related to the Tsar, after all. Instead he had the count and Sophie sit on either side of him. They insisted on having their personal bodyguards stand behind them. They were a trifle off-putting, two stern, shaven-headed men, arms folded over their high-collared shirts, baggy-trousered, booted, dagger in sash. Expressionless.

There was certainly no problem about grub. The army fare had been supplemented by the foreigners' own. He had rarely seen such an array of cosmestibles since leaving the east coast. And they had provided their own china, silverware and cutlery.

'Please help yourself, Princess,' he said, and pushed across a plate of quails' eggs. 'We don't stand on ceremony in this country.'

The count's English butler, a prissy little man in a black velvet suit and frilled shirt, frowned at him and leaned over with his white gloves to spoon a couple of the eggs on to Sophie's plate, along with some Beluga caviar from a silver dish.

'I wish to get hold of some reliable guides,' the count said, beckoning the butler to open a magnum of champagne. 'It possible is to have company of your men?'

'Well, no, sir, I'm afraid I've no authority for that,' the captain replied. 'I'd have to have notification. We're badly undermanned as it is. You see, we have thousands of square miles of Indian country to patrol. We've also got trouble on the frontiers.'

'Are we in *danger?*' Sophie squawked, the rubies of her necklace trembling on her bosom in the low-cut dress. 'Will the Indians attack?'

'No.' The captain took the liberty to pat her hand. It was a long time since he'd been in such close proximity to so attractive a young lady. 'Please don't distress yourself. The tribes around here are real friendly. Just as long as you confine your activities to the Wichita mountains. It's the most beautiful part of the Territory, the lakes full of fish, the woods teeming with wildlife.'

'I vould like to catch beaver, bear, antelope.' The count's white uniform was emblazoned with medals and be-jewelled decorations. He had babyish blond hair and pale-blue eyes. He looked a bit of a dreamer. 'I vant to take pelts, mount trophies. That permissible is?'

Princess Sophie giggled. 'Alexis wants to impress Father.' She raised the champagne and clinked glasses with Hazeltin. 'To your good fortune, Captain.'

'Call me Franklin,' he said, as his eyes met hers. 'To the hunt. I'm sure you'll have fun.'

'I want to shoot a buffalo.'

'That shouldn't be difficult. You might well come cross a herd if you go up through Blue Beaver Creek and along to Jedediah

Johnson Lake. But I must strictly warn you both that it would be unwise to venture out on to the plains into the area known as Old Greer County. That's where we've been having trouble with the Comanche. We are planning a punitive expedition against them. However'—he took the liberty to touch her hand again—'you should be quite safe among the lakes of the Wichita mountains.'

'I haff my men,' the count said, as he tucked into canned oysters. 'If zere is any trouble zey vill take care of us.'

'Hmm?' The captain eyed the two Cossacks. They sure looked fierce but he wasn't certain they would be a match for Comanche, or, for that matter, some of the varmints infesting Indian Territory. Before the war any white hunters had been required to pay a large fee for a licence to hunt. But since the war it was fast becoming a haven for renegades and outlaws escaping white man's justice. 'I hope your guards know how to shoot.'

'You better stock up on bullets,' one of his lieutenants, Matt Clay, advised. 'Our sutler's store is well-provided.'

Sophie smiled down the table at him, graciously. 'You look awfully smart in your uniform. I did not realize that people of your race could be officers.'

'Lieutenant Clay was one of the first Negro officers to pass out of West Point. We are a democratic country now,' the captain said.

'Yeah,' Clay grinned, with a hint of a sneer. 'We sho are officers and gen'lmen now. But I bet we go home on furlough they won't let us in white man's saloon.'

'It takes time,' Hazeltin said. 'What really bothers me, Princess, is the possibility of robbery. Those rubies around your neck' —his glance flickered upon her pale bosom —'they are exquisite, most becoming. And the matching bracelet and ring.' He picked up her hand to examine it. 'What a stone!'

Sophie allowed her hand to linger in

his. 'Indeed,' she trilled, laughingly. 'They are priceless. But they are not mine. My maternal grandmother, the Countess Ekterina, loaned them to me for this trip. We had to impress the people in Washington, you know.'

'Yes, but I really don't think you should flaunt them out here in the wilds. There are some very unscrupulous characters about.'

'Oh, foo, Captain! If you've got it, flaunt it, like you Americans say.'

'Perhaps it would be best if you left your valuables in safe custody here?'

'Oh, no. We always dress for dinner. I love to wear pretty things.'

'Do not vorry, Captain.' The count flipped his fingers. 'Ve have our own safe in ze vagon for us to lock in our valuables. Ve do not dress like zis during ze daytime.'

'That's good. I only wish I could come with you.' Franklin stared at the princess, his face going the colour of the pickled beetroot on the table, for he could hear the rustle of her dress as her thigh pressed against his knee. Was she doing it deliberately? Could she have had too much champagne? Her cheek dimpled as she glanced away, picked up her silver knife and fork and studied, with some disdain, the plate of steaming corned beef hash provided by the US Army cook as his contribution to the feast. 'I only wish I could,' he breathed.

'Vot is zis?' the count asked with dismay.

At first the captain thought he was referring to his ungentlemanly attentions to his sister, but it was only the corned beef. 'Oh—uh—traditional fare of our country.'

Was he mistaken? Was he going mad? Had he been too long out of decent society, deprived of the charms of the fair sex? Or was she rubbing her silk-stockinged ankle against his leg? This was a strange princess indeed.

Three

It was the Fall of the year, a faint chill in the air, and looking across from Scott Mountain, the highest point for miles, the countryside was a patchwork quilt of bright colours, auburns and yellows of the wooded slopes, blue lakes and winding river, verdant green meadows and rich red earth, the haze of hills stretching away into the distance. 'It sure is God's own country,' the Texan sighed, as he sat his horse and looked across it. 'There sure ain't no way they're gonna allow the red man to hang on to all this.' Already half of the Territory had been taken from the civilized tribes as punishment for supporting the Confederacy during the war. And he knew that white settlers were clamouring for the right to move into the area. Some already had, defying the government. 'Sooners' they called them, by way of meaning 'Sooner than later.' But Pete saw little sign of human habitation as he travelled on his way skirting the southern tips of Lost Lake, Lake Osage, around the great Quannah Parker water, across a buffalo plain to the north of Ketch Lake and down Blue Beaver Creek, a trail remembered from his days as a guerrilla leader.

He was surprised to see a cluster of new built log cabins on the far side of the creek and went splashing across on the grey, the paint back in her role as pack-horse.

A crudely painted sign said, 'Blue Beaver City'.

'Huh! Some city. Come on, gal, maybe we can git ye some split corn in this place. You've sure earned it.'

Any collection of shacks shoved together in the far West was generally given the title of city and this was a run-down hole if ever he'd seen one. Most of the cabins appeared to be shuttered and unoccupied, but there was a lean-to 'livery' and blue smoke was drifting from the tin chimney of the biggest cabin which bore the scrawled sign, 'Ebediah Pope—Trading Store'. Maybe he could get himself a hot meal. After weeks in the wilderness any sign of civilization was a welcome sight. It would make a change to eat indoors with his knees under a real table. Stiff from riding, he swung a leather-fringed leg over the saddle and jumped down. He hitched the grey mare and the paint filly, fondling their manes in a friendly fashion. 'You hang on here.' There were three scrubby ill-used broncs tied up outside. They looked like they'd been there a long time. A heap of rubbish, tin cans, offal and animal guts was piled up outside the cabin door. There were antlers and pelts tacked to the walls, an axe in a log; the owner didn't seem very houseproud. An Indian girl was chopping firewood. She glanced at him, her dark eyes sullen, expecting only insults or ill-treatment from a white man, and went on with her work. Wichita, he guessed, from the tattoos on her face and the design in black on her red blanket. 'Howdy,' he muttered, but she did not reply.

There was not much other sign of life on the city's mud street except for a few scrawny chickens pecking about. He wasn't expecting any trouble, but out of long habit, loosened his twin Smith and Wessons, pulling back his frock coat with its bullet scorches. The door creaked loudly as he pushed it open.

The cabin was dim, murky and musty with one window of bottleglass. It took a while for the Texan to accustom his eyes to the gloom but he made out three shadowy *hombres* sprawled on rough-hewn benches around the pot-belly stove. A portly man in a bowler hat and greasy suit was standing behind a makeshift bar. There were piles of blankets, barrels of hickory nuts and dried beans. 'Afternoon, gents,' Black Pete growled.

They had the air of being caught doing

something they didn't ought to and he knew what. An unmistakable tang of liquor filled the air. Liquor was banned from sale in the Indian Nations. It caused too much trouble. Pete's throat became constricted by the tantalizing scent. He hadn't had a drop since leaving Virginia City.

'What can I do for you, mistuh?'

'Same as you're doin' for these other three: a shot of whiskey.'

'Yeah? Who the hell you think you are comin' in here accusin' me?' Ebediah Pope looked like at one time he might have been a dude in a real city, but from the crumpled state of his suit and collarless shirt it was a long time ago. 'Where you sprung from, anyhow? You from Fort Sill?'

'No.' The Texan's voice was a husky whisper. 'The other direction: outa the wilderness. And I got a thirst on me.'

'You ain't one of them dang poky-nosed marshals?'

'Nope. Nor a gimp, neither.' Leastways

he wasn't any longer. He had recently been both US marshal at Virginia City and bounty hunter, but it didn't do to tell them that. 'Jest a weary traveller headin' home, thassall.'

'Hey-yee!' one of the men hooted. 'We gotten ourselves a real Confederate offee-saw. What d'ye know, boys. We're rich!' He jerked up a rifle from beneath the bench and covered the Texan. 'You know who this is? Black Pete Bowen, leader of the Cherokee Light Cavalry. Fought against the Union. Carried on guerrilla attacks after the peace. I see-d him once down along Lake Lawtonka with his men. Watch him, boys. He's faster than a rattler.'

The Texan's face split into a grin and he placed his hands on the bar. 'Very flattering of you, suh, to remember me. It's true the handle's Black Pete, at least, that's what they used to call me. Hate to disappoint you, but there ain't no ree-ward on me. I took the oath of allegiance a year ago.'

'Yeah, who you kiddin'?' The man with the rifle was wearing a topcoat three sizes too big for him, and a heavy Stetson. All that could be seen of his face above his beard was a ruddy stub of nose and two little red eyes glimmering greedily in the squinting beams of sunlight. 'Why you still wearin' that uniform with them fancy doodahs?'

He poked the longarm at the Austrian braid-knots denoting first lieutenant on Pete Bowen's sleeve. His two sidekicks had pulled long-barrelled revolvers from their belts and gawped at him. One was an older man, a bag of bones and parchment in a mangy fur. He was bald, with no teeth, except for one twisted fang at the front. The other was a big, blond galoot in a lumberjack shirt. He would have been handsome but the smallpox had eaten away half his face.

'They wouldn't have given you no pardon,' the man with the rifle drawled. 'They would have made you kick air. You raise them hands nice and slow now. Don't try no fancy tricks.'

'Heck, I'm gittin' tired of this. War's been over nigh on two years now. I took the oath up in Nevada, more civilized parts. You wanna see it? I got it in my pocket. I wear this coat for old time's sake. Kinda got attached to it.'

'Yeah? Easy!' The rifle jerked back with alarm as Pete reached inside his frock coat. 'Whaddya doin'?'

'Jest gonna show you the damn paper, dim brain.' Pete carefully drew the oath of allegiance signed by the previous marshal in Virginia City from his inside pocket. 'Put your peepers on that.'

'Duh?' The piggy eyes stared at the ornate form. He passed it to Ebediah. 'You can figure words, cain't ya?'

The trader pulled out wire-rimmed spectacles to squint at the piece of paper and beamed at them. 'Boys, looks like the real thang. Put them guns away. You been causing the stranger undue hassle. So, what's it to be Mistuh Bowen?'

'Same as what you're having,' Pete gave the three roughnecks a wry grimace. 'And what you got by way of eats? I'm ravenous.'

Ebediah went under the counter to turn a tap on a barrel and came up with a tumbler of copper-coloured whiskey. 'We're clean out of fresh meat. Or salt pork, too. All I can do you is beans.'

'Beans! I sure had my fill of beans. How about that rooster outside?'

Ebediah took an axe and thunked it into the bar top. 'You catch it, kill it, pluck it, gut it, I'll cook it.'

'Gimme some corn for my broncs.' Pete sampled the whiskey warily. It rolled around his tongue and burned his throat, sending a fierce glow shuddering through him. 'Whoo! Real corn lightning.'

'Sure is. Made it myself.' Ebediah handed him a bucket of oats and two nosebags. 'There y'are.'

'Give these scurvy rats one on me,' Pete

drawled. 'To show there ain't no hard feelin's.'

He went out to see to the horses. The Indian girl was sitting on the stoop huddled in her blanket against the cold wind. 'Loosen up,' he grinned. 'It'll soon be Christmas. Wichita?'

She nodded, her broad, high-cheekboned face impassive.

'Thought so.' He went back in. The three dingbats were knocking back the whiskey looking flushed and high-spirited. Pete swallowed the remains of his, and knocked the glass for a refill. 'Don't I know you?' he asked the man in the Stetson. 'Jake McGinty? The Gunpowder Man?'

'That's me. I went on a little expedition with you and your boys. Don't you remember, Lootenant? Blew the safe for you when you raided Fort Washita.'

'Mad Jake, the explosives expert. You got a damn nerve tryin' to turn me in for the bounty.'

'I'm a mercenary, not a Confederate. Man's got to make a living. Where you been hiding the past year, Loo-tenant?'

'Like I said, up in Nevada.'

'You bin makin' yourself a fortune diggin' fer gold?'

'A fool's errand. All the smart operators from California have moved in.' Pete lit a cheroot and tried not to show he was thinking about the $3,000 'fortune' stashed in his paint's backpack. 'By the time I got there the big mining companies had taken over. There weren't nuthin' left fer the small man. I'm goin' back to Texas, raise a few cows.'

'Yeah; You got yourself a good grub-stake?' the almost toothless old cur wheezed.

'I sure ain't. Like I said, I wasted my time. Think I'd have come back overland if I had? I'd have gone in style, railroad and steamboat.'

'Sure is a damn long way to trail,' Ebediah mused. 'More'n thousand miles.

How'd you come?'

'Took the old pony express trail across to Salt Lake City and cut south down to Green City. Crossed the Colorado where it's no more than a muddy stream. Through the desert and the Canyon Lands to Pagosa Spring. Met some Navaho and Cheyenne but they're peaceful. When I got to Santa Fe I restocked and went up out through the Glorietta Pass. Took the old trail across the Panhandle following the upper reaches of the River Arkansas, and here I am back in the Nations. Had a spot of bother out on the plains 'fore I got here. Ran into a bunch of Comanche renegades. They weren't gonna let me pass, but after I killed a dozen of 'em they saw sense.'

'A dozen?' McGinty spluttered. 'Howdja do that?'

'With my guns. Howdja think?' Pete took another swallow of whiskey and his black eyes smouldered as he studied the curling cigar smoke. 'It was a real badass Comanch' called Red Bone.'

'Red Bone!' Pope exclaimed. 'You shoulda brought him in. There sure is a price on his scalp.'

The three dingbats eyed the Texan uneasily as he threw off the heavy grey greatcoat and stretched, lean and broad-shouldered, in his blue cross-over canvas shirt, red bandanna, shotgun chaps, and ivory-handled .32s slung low. He didn't look like a young man to tangle with.

'How come you not head south down Panhandle?' the rawboned Swede asked.

'Because I didn't want to run into any more Comanch' war parties. I'm gonna follow the Chisholm Trail down to Southern Texas. At least the Injins round here are civilized.'

'If,' Ebediah smirked, 'you can call any savage civilized.'

'The Cherokee were by way of being my friends,' the Texan muttered, darkly. He pulled the axe out of the bar top. 'I guess I'll go git me Mister Rooster.' He gulped back the last in the glass and the liquor rasped through him, making his head swirl. 'A mite rough but I've had worse. Don't drink it all 'fore I git back.'

'Guaranteed to send you mad as a coon,' Ebediah cackled. 'You'll be lucky you catch that bird. He goes like a road runner.'

'I'll catch him,' he grunted, testing the axe blade on his palm. 'I woulda shot myself a durn buffalo if I'd known. Passed a tidy herd way back.'

But it wasn't as easy as that. When the rooster eyed him staggering out of the cabin, a tad unsteady with the axe, he set off on his long legs. Pete whooped and raced after him. At the end of the street the canny fowl did a rapid U-turn and hared back again. Through the cabin window they saw Pete go past hot on his heels. 'He ain't got a chance,' Jeb guffawed.

'Take a look in his coat. That boy ain't rode all the way to Virginia City and back all fer nuthin'. He's got gold on him.'

'No cash in here,' Jeb said, riffling

through the pockets. 'Must have hid it some place.'

'I tell ya he's got plenty gold on him,' Mad Jake said. 'I can smell it. An' we gonna git our mitts on it. But we gotta be careful. Like I said that boy's got true Texan instincts. Shoot first ask questions later.'

'Boys,' Ebediah crooned out, filling another bottle from the barrel. 'I ain't listening to this.'

'We kin handle him,' Jeb wheezed, priming a long-barrelled buffalo gun.

After chasing the cock twice round the cabin Pete changed tack and hurled himself at one of the hens. He made a grab and a dive slithering in the mud. It squawked and fluttered from his grasp, flapping its wings as if to take flight. The whiskey did not help. His knees had gone weak and his mind wavered as he tried to coax another to him. It croaked and scurried off. The rooster stood watching him with his beady eyes, ruddy chopped with indignation, shaking his gaudy tail feathers. Pete chased after him again, tripped over a feed trough, landed on his backside, his hat over his eyes ...

The Indian girl smiled broadly, took an armful of wood and went inside.

'Waal, lookee who's here,' the pock-faced youngster crowed. 'The li'l squaw. I could sure do with a taste of her.'

'Yeah.' The old one grinned his gummy fang. 'Go git her, boy.'

Mad Jake's arm crooked around her throat, dragging her back. The Wichita girl shrieked and kicked out, dropping the logs. Mad Jake's hairy-jawed whiskey breath was in her face. The pox-eaten Swede's filthy hands were groping at her skirts, pulling apart her legginged legs. 'No, mistuh,' she begged, 'please.'

'Give it to her,' the fanged one yelled.

'Boys,' Ebediah said. 'I don't think this is a good idea. I'll have to put her on your bill.'

'You shut up,' Mad Jake grunted, his Stetson falling off to show his greasy hair. 'We all whiskied up and we gonna have us some fun.'

Outside Pete was puzzled. 'How the hell does anyone ever git his hands on one of these thangs?' He decided to use caution. Most of the flustered birds had hurried off to a scraggy pine, flapping up into its branches where, no doubt, they perched all night. 'Aha! They got a roosting tree.' He would have to be like a prairie fox. Sneak up on 'em. He crouched low and on tiptoe stealthily dodged from rock to rock up around the tree, stumbling when the whiskey made him miss his judgement. He parted the needles and peered up. There they were, the varmints. He hauled on a branch and leapt upwards. 'Ouch!' His head cracked with a coconut sound on wood. But he hung on to a kicking claw. He'd got one. He pulled it from the pine and quickly twisted its neck. It was only a hen but she would do. He took her round the back of the cabin to gut and pluck.

When he pushed open the cabin door, victoriously holding aloft the featherless fowl with its bloody headless stump, he stared with surprise. The dirty bastards were down on the floor, whooping and growling, giving it to the Indian gal. 'What's goin' on here?' he asked, though, with the Swede's bare hams shuddering and Mad Jake sitting on her head it was pretty obvious. 'Leave her be.'

'You jest keep outa this,' the gummy one snarled from behind him and Pete felt the business end of a Sharps buffalo gun poked in his side.

'This ain't right,' Pete dropped the bird. He gripped the rifle barrel and thrust it aside as it exploded, ear-shatteringly. He klonked the bald-pate with the axe in his left hand, sending him tumbling to the floor.

The Swede looked back with alarm, as if reluctant to stop. Pete grabbed at his coat collar and hauled him off. He jabbed with the axe, knocking his teeth down his throat, and hurled him out of the open door.

Mad Jake was crouched over the girl, going for his revolver. Pete threw the axe at him, knocking the gun from his hand. Mad Jake cursed and sucked at his torn knuckles. Pete pulled him up, spun him over to the door, and slammed a right into his jaw. Jake went back-kicking out to land in the mud.

Pete got hold of the older man, who was groaning, and feeling at his bloody head. He propelled him to the door and tossed him out on to the other two. The Swede was reaching for his side-arm. 'I wouldn't if I were you.' Pete had his twin Smith and Wessons out aimed unerringly at them. 'Toss that gun away. Now y'all git on your durn hosses and git outa here 'fore I lose my temper.'

They scrambled to their horses, ugly leers on their faces. They helped the old guy on to his as he moaned and clutched at his bleeding head. 'What are you, a lousy Injin-lover?' Mad Jake sneered.

'I see you back here I'll kill you,' Pete whispered. 'Git goin'.'

He blazed away about the horses' hoofs, making them kick and whinny, and go galloping away, the men hanging on to them. He loosed three more shots about their heads for good measure.

'Phew!' he said, calming his own horses. 'Dirty low-down polecats. They got me all shook up.'

The Wichita girl was still on the floor, dazed, rearranging her clothing. 'Good job I hit him with the back of that axe,' Pete grinned. 'I mighta killed him. He's gonna have a hangover for a week or two, that's for sure.'

Ebediah shook his head and presented him with another tumbler of whiskey. 'Look at my wall,' he said, staring at the gaping hole where the buffalo slug had blasted through. 'Who's gonna pay me fer that?'

'Aw, put it on the bill,' Pete drawled, soothing himself with the corn lightning. 'Now how about that chicken? My guts is groaning.'

'Mad Jake ain't gonna like this.'

'Hell take him. I'll have a meal, load up some supplies and be on my way. He don't worry me.'

Ebediah began chopping up the chicken and stirred the pieces in a pan of flour, bear grease and onions. When the girl tried to help him he shouted at her, 'Get away! Go on. Clear out. I've had enough of you. You're more trouble than you're worth.'

'You OK?' Pete asked her.

She met his eyes, nodded, and went into a back room. She came out with a blanket roll. There was a look of pain in her eyes as she felt her abdomen.

'They hurt you?' He went to the pan, fished out a leg and a couple of bits that looked cooked. 'Here, put these into your pocket. No need to starve, too.'

The girl took them, wrapped them in

a piece of cotton rag. Without speaking, she went out of the cabin, shutting the door, quietly. When he looked out of the window she was heading away towards the woods.

He sat down to eat his meal and shook his head. Nothing had changed. 'Don't know why I get so het up,' he muttered. 'She's only a damn Injin after all.'

Four

Black Pete woke in the hay of the livery where he had slept the night. 'Aw, jeez,' he groaned as he sat up. 'My head!' He was full-dressed, his hat crammed over his eyes. His gunbelt lay close at hand. 'Fat lot of good they would have done me,' he muttered, as he stood, groggily, and buckled the S & Ws back on. 'Slept like the dead. That red-eye sure knocked me out.'

The grey and paint shuffled in the hay and watched him, disapprovingly, as if to say, 'Time we was on our way.'

'Sure, it's all right for you,' he said. 'You don't drink, do you? Take my advice, stick to clear fresh water.'

He went to his big pack and delved a hand inside. For moments his heart thudded, thinking it had gone. But, no, the tarpaulin-covered package was still there containing the greenbacks, silver dollars and pouches of gold dust.

Old Ebediah was to be trusted, after all. Instead of journeying on as planned, Pete had hit the bottle and browsed the evening away beside the stove. Much against his better judgement he had bedded down in the stable. He had half-expected the rats—the human ones—to come sneaking back.

'Marnin'.' He pushed into the trading store. 'Just gimme a coffee, black, hot and sweet.'

'We had a visitor in the night,' Ebediah said. 'You lose anything?'

'Nope. Don't believe I did. What's wrong?'

'The buffalo rifle's gone. I reckon old Jeb must have come back for it: 'twere his prize possession. Musta crept in through that hole in the wall. I didn't hear a thing.'

'I'd 'a thought that crack on the head would have deterred him.'

'He's crazy. They all are. You better watch your back on the trail.'

'Mm,' Pete mumbled, holding his pounding brow. 'I surely will. Wouldn't like to be on the receivin' end of that weapon. It could part a man's head from his shoulders.'

He paid his bill, saddled up, and loaded his rig tight on the paint. 'So long,' he called, and followed the shallow stream along through the high-walled Blue Beaver Creek.

He kept a sharp lookout but didn't see a soul. After an hour's ride he stopped and watched the antics of some beavers building their lodge. Why anyone should want to slaughter those clever little animals wholesale he didn't know. But their numbers had been decimated due to the trade in beaver furs and top hats. Fortunately, the latter had become unfashionable. Mind you, he was mighty partial to beaver tail stew. But he resisted the temptation to pot one for himself. He had spent three years in the company of the Cherokee during the war and some of their respect for the animals and the natural world must have brushed off on him. Anyhow, his head ached, and his guts were churning from the sourmash. Never again! He contented himself scooping a hatful of water to drink, and went on his way.

'Here he comes now,' Mad Jake hissed, squinting along the sights of his carbine as the lanky, straight-backed Texan ambled towards them with his two horses.

'Where?' Jeb, the one-fanged one, climbed down beside him to get a better look. He only had a revolver and the Texan was out of range. 'Let him get nearer. We wanta make sure of this.'

'We make sure,' the Swede gritted out through the bloody broken stumps of his teeth. 'Don't you worry about that.' He, too, trained a carbine on the cowboy—a Spencer seven-shot.

They had chosen their spot well, high on a ledge above the creek. They had left their broncs further along below the cliff, where Blue Beaver Creek emerged into rolling plain.

'Now!' Mad Jake had his sights on the Texan's shirt directly over his heart. He squeezed out a slug, and the Swede began firing, too. The Texan was blasted from his horse to lay outstretched on the pebbles of the creek. 'Got him!' Mad Jake shouted.

Pete knew only a burning sensation in his chest as the bullet pounded into him, toppling him from the saddle. The explosions echoed through the canyon, and his horses skittered away on down the creek in fright.

'Hot shee-it!' To go all through the war, and to end like this—bushwhacked. You're going to die, a voice in his head told him. It's all over. It was as if he was slipping out of his body, standing, looking down at himself. This is it, he thought. But then, as bullets spattered about him, another voice deep in his subconscious, said, No. Hang on. Fight it. He tried to claw for his Smith and Wessons but a red mist, the colour of blood, flowed over him, filling his eyes ...

'He's dead,' the Swede said, his Spencer empty.

'Let's go down make sure,' Jeb growled. 'I want my buffalo gun back.'

'Yeah,' Mad Jake agreed. 'Put a coupla more slugs in him.'

As they showed themselves and began to climb down the cliffside an explosion clapped out from the cliff on the opposite side and a bullet whistled past their heads, taking away a chunk of the cliff. They scrambled back for their lives.

'Whew!' Jeb wheezed. 'That's my damn buffalo gun. An' whoever's up there knows how to use it.'

'Yeah,' the Swede agreed. 'He got hisself a friend.'

'There's no gettin' down to him. We'd be sittin' ducks.' Mad Jake took a couple of pot shots across at where the puff of smoke had come from, but to no avail. 'Less go git his hosses. See what he was carryin'. He's dead, sho' 'nough.'

'Maybe,' the Swede suggested, 'we could get up round back of whoever is over there. It take time to reload buff'lo gun.'

'Nah.' Jeb's voice quavered. 'Mebbe it's one of them marshals. Jake's right. Less git. He can have the gun.'

As another buffalo slug took the top of their rock away they scrambled back down the way they had come, back to their broncs, and set off after the escaped horses. The grey, however, had turned back up the creek, tentatively nosing back towards the man who had cared for her. They only managed to catch the paint.

'Hey, look at this!' Mad Jake hooted, as he tore open the tarpaulin package and silver dollars and wads of notes tumbled out. 'I knew he was lying.'

'My God!' The Swede stared in awe. 'We really rich this time.'

And Jeb, in spite of his bandaged head, did a little jig of joy on the sand.

The dark curtain seemed to be raised from Pete's eyes and he was back in the realm of pain. A rough tongue was licking at his face and he looked up into the grey's bearded, yellow-toothed jaw. 'Aw, hell,' he groaned, for it hurt to move. Someone was nudging him, gently shaking his arm and he saw the Indian girl, her dark, moon-shaped face, her concerned eyes.

'Mistuh, you gotta wake up.' And then she spoke in her own language, words different to Cherokee, but he understood her. 'I am going to help you.'

She eased out his long Bowie knife, sharp as a razor, and looked down at him, fiercely. She pushed a bit of smooth driftwood between his teeth. 'Bite on this.' He nearly broke his teeth as he did so, and the knife went in. Pain like a bolt of lightning shuddered through him. She, too, gritted her teeth as she probed the wound. 'Got it,' she said, fishing out the big slug.

Pete breathed a sigh of relief thinking that the worst pain had ceased: there was more to come. She tipped gunpowder from a horn on to the open wound, took his tin of matches from his shirt pocket and struck one. The gunpowder ignited with a hiss. Aagh!' Pete could not help crying out. But he knew she had cauterized the wound. What was she doing now? She had got him under the arms and was trying to drag him into the river. 'What are you doin'?' he gasped out.

'Water good.' She pushed him face first into the shallows. He lay there and let the freezing water wash away his blood. The girl looked back, fearfully, over her shoulder. She laid his Smith and Wesson close at hand in case they returned. 'Mistuh,' she said urgently, pulling him back. 'We gotta go.'

'Yeah.' He was breathing hard and shivering. 'You're a good kid.'

For the first time she smiled, a white-toothed smile that lit up her face. 'You good to me. Me good to you. I try to get you on horse.'

First she wetted his bandanna and tried to staunch the blood. 'You hang on to that. Come on, you gotta get up.'

'Yeah,' he gasped, and with an almighty effort forced himself on to his knees. He hung on to her as she pulled him up, and somehow managed to get a toe in the stirrup, a hand on the saddle horn, and swung up into the saddle. He sat swaying on the grey, the mist threatening to close over him again. 'Where we goin'?' he muttered.

'A friend.' She took the reins and led him back up the creek, stepping lightly, the way that Indians did.

Five

Bullets, rifles, bourbon, wine, cigars, flour and basic foodstuffs were ordered by Count Alexis and Princess Sophie when they visited the sutler's store at Fort Sill.

'Vill you put it on my bill?' the count said, airily, as the bald-pated sutler totted up what he owed.

'On your bill? What bill?' He raised an enquiring eyebrow at the young captain who was accompanying them. 'How long you gonna be here?'

'Oh, many veeks. I vill write you a Vells Fargo cheque for presentation at ze bank in Fort Gibson.' He did so with a flourish. 'There ve are.'

The sutler studied the signature, mightily impressed, and Sophie produced a wad of dollar bills from her bag to purchase some boiled sweets and cans of lemonade. The bills were newly pressed, almost difficult to part from each other.

'Ve could pay it all in cash but ve vill need notes to pay ze guides and any other incidentals,' the count smiled.

'Of course,' Captain Hazeltin agreed. 'I am sure that will be all right. Our sutler will have to take a trip to Fort Gibson soon to get more supplies.'

'Really, when will that be?' Sophie asked, rather sharply.

'Not before the end of the month. Why do you ask?'

'Good. I just thought by then we will have finished our hunting and we could head back with him. We had some difficulty finding our way here.'

Sophie was still wearing her rubies and the taffeta dress of the night before, perhaps wanting to look her best for the handsome officer. She smiled up at him and said, 'Our ship docked at New Orleans, you know, the port, and we came up the

Mississippi on a huge riverboat. We transferred to a smaller steamboat and went up the Arkansas. After Fort Smith it was more difficult, the Webber Falls, and other rapids, but your flat-bottoms are ideal. There were numerous paddle-ships tied up at the quayside when we reached Fort Gibson.'

'It's become a very busy place since the war,' Hazeltin said. 'The centre of all routes in the Territory. I thought you said you visited Washington?'

'Ah, yes, that was before. We took ship round from Savannah to New Orleans. Such fun!'

'You're having quite a trip, Princess. Now we must look to finding you some guides.' The Russian servants were loading the supplies on to the wagons and Captain Hazeltin strode out to the muddy parade ground. As he did so he spied three men riding through the open gates of the stockade. 'I wonder who they are?'

'Zoze men, zey look like hunters to me.

Maybe ve can hire zem?'

'A rather disreputable bunch.' Hazeltin was immaculate in his double-breasted dark-blue uniform with its shiny gilt buttons, gold epaulettes and flashes. 'But in this country you never can tell.'

'They must know the countryside,' Princess Sophie said. 'Ask them if they will be our guides.'

'Yes, ve do not vish to be lost,' the count agreed.

'You men!' the captain shouted. 'Come over here.' They certainly looked a surly bunch as they paused, slouched in their saddles, their carbines under their arms. But, being new to the area he had not met them before, and one had to take a man on face value. 'You will have to show them who's boss. Don't take any cheek from them. These backwoodsmen are a rum lot.'

'Of course,' Sophie laughed, as the men walked their horses over to them.

'Yeah?' A bearded one in an overlarge

overcoat and Stetson glowered at them. 'What you want?'

'What do *you* want is more to the point?' The captain eyed them, haughtily. 'What are you doing here?'

'We come to buy stores from the sutler's and renew our licence to hunt. We got cash to pay.'

'See, they *are* hunters.' Sophie clapped her hands with delight. 'You men, would you like to work for my brother?'

'Work fer him?' Jeb bared his fang at the little blond-bearded man in the funny topcoat and military hat. 'What we wanna work fer him fer? We don't need money. We got plenty.'

'Shut up,' Mad Jake said. 'I do the talkin' in this outfit.'

The Swede stared open-mouthed at Sophie, her rings and necklace, leaned across, nudged Jake and whispered something.

'I seen 'em,' he muttered. 'Doncha worry.' He raised his voice to the captain.

'Who are you people?'

'I am in command of this post. This is His Royal Highness Count Alexis, relative of the Tsar of Russia, and this is his sister, Princess Sophie. They plan to go hunting among the Wichita lakes and hills. They need guides. I am sure they will pay well.'

'They will, will they?' Jake screwed up his eyes, and tried not to grin at his good fortune. 'Waal, mebbe we could help 'em out. Nobody knows this Territory like we does.'

'Yeh.' Jeb started giggling, almost drooling, as he looked at the blonde girl. 'Nobody does.'

'I must warn you, you will be in charge of their safety. They have their personal bodyguards. But, if anything should happen to their highnesses there would be international repercussions.'

'Reaper-what?' Jeb echoed.

'Kusshuns. You heard him.' Jake began to laugh. 'Doncha worry about that, Cap.

We'll look after them jest fine. Russkies, eh? Waal, whadda ya know!' He spat a gob of tobacco juice to land by the princess's high-heel bootees. 'Jest fancy.'

'Nobody will get at 'em past us,' the Swede grinned. 'We know the Injins, we know the land good.'

'I think you would be advised to bear in mind what I say. If anything unfortunate should occur there would be no place you could hide, nowhere in the whole world.'

'Sho, you can depend on us, Cap.' Jake gave a one-fingered salute to his Stetson. 'We are well known fer our honesty. Honest Jake they call me.'

'And another thing, you should address them as your highness and milady.'

'Which one's which?' Jake said, wiping his eyes and smiling at the count. 'Milady.'

That set off the other two laughing again. 'You can go help them load their supplies,' Captain Hazeltin snapped.

As the three horsemen turned away to ride over to the wagons Mad Jake hissed,

'Boys, this is our lucky day. Look at this, real French champagne. We gonna have a party.'

The Swede looked uncertain. 'But what of that captain say? That we would have no place to hide?'

'Pah,' Jeb scoffed. 'This is a big country.'

'Yeah, you see the size of the rubies round that gal's neck? That's apart from all this other stuff. We'll take 'em along to Frenchman's Lake. Nobody'll find 'em for weeks. By that time we'll have drifted down to Arizon-ey. I'm gittin' tired of this Territ'ry.'

'Yeah, bejesus,' Jeb cried. 'I'll have enough to retire, open me own saloon. There's only them two guys in the fur hats to take care of.'

'Sure,' the Swede muttered. 'They be no trouble. But it sure is risky. Me, I take my cut and go on, right on down to Mexico. I open my own silver mine.'

'Yeah, jest think of them li'l señoritas!'

Mad Jake looked across at his new employers. 'Jest think of that li'l princess. You see the titties on her? Whoo-whee! I cain't wait to git my hands on her.'

Over at the captain's cabin Sophie was saying a lingering goodbye. 'I do wish you could come with us, Franklin. While I am in your country I want to behave like ... like a democratic woman, away from all the ties of being royalty. I want to hunt and fish in the lakes and ride and be free. Do you understand?'

'Yes, I think I do.' The young captain held on to her dainty gloved hand. Her perfume was overpowering. Her touch, her blue-eyed gaze made his head spin. He felt more scared than before a battle. 'I do. I will come to look for you in a week's time to make sure you are happy. Sophie, I promise, we will ... we will ride together.'

'How heavenly! I will hold you to that. I must go now.'

He raised her gloved hand to his lips, clicked his boot heels and bowed stiffly from the waist. 'To next week,' he said, and watched her go wiggling away.

Six

He was spinning back in time, the eyeless dead of Shiloh rising to their knees again, their supplicating hands reaching for him, back to before the war, his teenage days in the dark woods of east Texas, the first man he had ever killed, the Comanche galloping towards him, tomahawk raised. So many dead, so many he had sent to the Other Side: he did not know there were so many. And here they were waiting for him in the Vale of Shadows. No! Not yet! He struggled to escape, twisting and turning, calling out, but his strength had gone and they were beckoning to him. For endless nights, it seemed, he lived in this Other Land ...

Suddenly he surfaced, as if rising from the bottom of a dark lake and burst into sunshine, gasping for air, looking about him, as if he was reborn. 'Where am I?' He figured he must be in a tipi made of buffalo hides for he could see blue sky through the smoke hole. An old Indian with white hair was swaying back and forth on his haunches waving a green ostrich feather, occasionally tossing a handful of red dust over him, and making a keening, high-pitched caterwauling.

'Who'n hell are you?' Pete croaked out. 'Fer Christ's sake quit that din.'

Whether he understood him or not the old man ceased his wailing when he saw the white man open his eyes and speak. He smiled, widely, gave another ululating cry of triumph up to the smoke hole. 'You have been on a long journey,' he said in Wichita. 'Welcome back.'

At least, that was what his words sounded like to Pete, although he wasn't too familiar with the Caddoan lingo. He was fluent in Cherokee, but they had been brought to the Territory from the far east coast, Carolina way, and their tongue was Iroquian. The Wichitas hailed from closer at hand, just north of the Kansas border. They were a very different branch of the aboriginal tree. However, the young Texan had tried to familiarize himself with as many different Indian languages as possible. He figured it to be as necessary for survival as carrying a brace of six-shooters.

'Any chance of a drink?' Pete whispered. 'My throat's as dry as a Sunday mornin'.'

The old Indian, dressed in worn buckskins, got to his feet and, giving a last wave of the ostrich feather, left the tipi. Pete tried to move but gave a gasp of pain. He raised the blanket and peered down at the wound in his chest. It looked a mess, covered in some kind of leaves and unguent. He was surprised to see he was naked.

'Whaddja done with my pants?' he asked, as the old man returned, accompanied by the girl.

'She wash them. They stank. All white

men stink. She wash you, too. Now you no stink.' The old man gave him a crafty grin. 'She like what she see.'

'Yeah? She did, did she? Well, that's my personal property.'

'Take no notice of my grandfather.' The girl spoke in her own language and raised a drinking horn of water to his lips. 'Here, drink.'

'What do you mean take no notice? I brought him back to life, didn't I? This feather has strong medicine.'

The water tasted better than whiskey, better than anything he had ever tasted, and he lay back and let it flow through him. He felt strangely peaceful, especially when the girl gently put her hand on his brow. It was like the calming touch of his mother when he was a child. 'You lot sure are fond of washing,' he said. 'Durn liberty, if you ask me.'

'The fever has gone. For many days you have been shouting, having visions.'

'Many days?' And then the memory

came flooding back to him. He tried to sit up again, the pain searing through him. 'My pack-hoss, the paint? You got her?'

'They took her. Those three bad men. We have your grey.'

'Gawn? Oh, my God! A year's striving, mining, marshaling, wasted. My stake. Three thousand dollars. I gotta git after 'em. How long I been here? Days, you say?'

'You must stay. Eat. Regain your strength. Take it a step at a time. You lost much blood.'

'The dirty, lousy, bushwhacking skunks. I gotta go git 'em.' But he knew it was true what she said. He felt as weak as a kitten. If he moved too suddenly there was a danger of the wound opening. 'How about my guns? I got twenty gold eagles stitched in the back of the belt.'

'We have your guns safe, Black Pit.'

'I guess you're right. I gotta rest up. I'll pay you.'

A look of disgust crossed the girl's

broad, bronzed countenance. 'We don't want your gold.'

'We are Wichita,' the grandfather said. 'Do not insult us. You are our guest.'

'I'm sorry. I didn't mean—uh—I guess you saved my life.'

The Indian girl was dressed in a white woman's blouse of paisley scrolls beneath her red blanket with its white geometrical design. She had leather leggings beneath her buckskin skirt, decorated down each side with little bells, which tinkled as she moved. Her shiny black hair was drawn back to reveal the curious tattoos on her cheeks, and she had large bone earrings. She gave a wistful smile and said, 'Grandfather's medicine brought you back.'

'No, it was Hole-in-Shoe saved you. She a damn good shot. She stole man's buffalo gun. Made them robbers run.'

'I saw what they were planning to do, that's all.'

'Well, I guess I'm lucky to be alive.

Thanks to you both. Hole-in-the-Shoe. Why they call you that?'

The grandfather grinned, wrinkles cracking his wizened visage. 'She is a bad girl, that's why. Her people have cast her out. No Wichita youth will take her for squaw. She is not pure.'

The girl lowered her lashes and stared at the ground. 'No,' she murmured, as if in pain.

'When she was young she went to hang around the forts. Many Indians are bewitched by white man's things, their beads, their baubles. How many times did you have to do it to get those little bells, Hole-in-Shoe?'

'No,' she pleaded. 'Do not tell him this.'

'Her father, my son, would not have her back. So she goes to live with Ebediah. He treat her bad. Now he has thrown her out, too. I am an old man. I cannot hunt much any more. What am I to do with her?'

'Aw, no,' the Texan groaned. The Indian

was peering down his aquiline nose at him in a very cunning manner. 'I got a girl waitin' fer me in Texas. You ain't off-loadin' her on me.'

'Off-loadin'? What you mean?'

'I mean I don't need no squaw. I'm grateful, don't get me wrong. Just git me my clothes and my guns and I'll be on my way.'

'Stay.' She put out her hand to him. 'Grandfather does not mean anything. I have no claim on you.'

'Yeah, well, I'm sorry, Hole—what did they call you 'fore you went bad.'

'Spotted Frog. One like that leapt on my mother's foot when she was giving me birth.'

'You don't say? So your people ain't around these parts?'

'No, they are in winter quarters up along Frenchman's Lake.'

He reached out and squeezed her hand. 'Must be kinda lonesome bein' an exile. Doncha worry, gal, some young brave won't be able to resist them brown eyes of yourn one of these days.'

'I go get you something to eat,' she said, and, shortly after, returned with a mess of meat in grease, which looked suspiciously like dog, and almost turned his stomach.

'He might even git used to your cookin',' Pete muttered. 'Though I cain't think I ever would.'

Seven

The four covered wagons of Count Alexis went out of Fort Sill rattling their precious cargo of fine wines, connoisseur foods and cut glasses and headed up Medicine Creek and out through rough, wooded country beneath the towering peak of Mount Signal. The count and Sophie rode their thoroughbreds, delighting in the crisp Fall weather, the hills a patchwork of differing hues, keeping a lookout for big game, unaware that they, themselves, had become the prey.

'We'll let 'em think they're havin' a good time,' Mad Jake McGinty muttered to his sidekicks. 'Hustle 'em along, boys. We wanna git as far away as possible from the fort. Mebbe we can make it look like we was attacked by Injins? Scalp 'em all.'

'Yep.' Jeb chortled through his gums. 'I'm gonna enjoy doin' that to that fat-assed li'l bossy butler. Look at him sat up on that wagon. Who's he think he is?'

They kept the wagons moving until they reached the shore of West Lake where they set up camp. The count had a silver inlaid James Purdy shotgun, made to measure, he said, by the famous English firm, with a stock of polished walnut and long barrel of engraved Damascus iron. The Oxford Street firm had provided a bullet mould and gunpowder flask, similarly well wrought, all in a polished case lined with green baize. The count ran out to take a shot at a v-shaped skein of geese which went honking by above headed for warmer climes. He bagged one for the pot. It fluttered and plunged into the lake and the huge, clipped French poodle, bred for hunting, waded in to retrieve it.

Sophie clapped her hands with delight as the count brandished his catch. The servants were putting up their tent and laying a trestle table with silverware, which the count took from a small safe he kept in his wagon. He took out the princess's rubies and a diamond tiara for her to wear at dinner. Mad Jake squinted in the back flap trying to see what else he had in there. 'It's one of them combination locks,' he reported, 'I seen them sort before. It won't be no trouble.'

They watched their employers strolling by the lake shore as their supper was made ready, the count pointing out a colony of cormorants on a rock. The falling sun, as it seeped away behind the mountains imbued the water the colour of blood. Sophie was holding on to her brother's arm, waving her other hand, rapturously. 'Them two's livin' in seventh heaven,' Jake growled, 'but they soon gonna git a rude awakening.'

'Heck, will you guess what?' the Swede told them. 'The princess only wants me to heat up a tin tub of water for her bath.'

'Bath?' Jeb displayed his fang with

dismay. 'This time of year? What is she, crazy?'

'Crazy? They both must be. You see that gun of his'n? That silver inlay? Must be worth a thousand dollars, if not more. That gun's gonna be mine.' Mad Jake watched the Swede carefully heft the hot water from the fire into the princess's tent, and back out bowing. 'That stoopid Swede's taking his services seriously.' He listened to squeals and splashing going on behind the canvas and gave a big wink. 'C'mon. Less take a peek.'

Making sure nobody was watching Mad Jake and Jeb tiptoed up to the square-rigged tent. Jake pulled his knife and carefully slit the canvas a little way. 'Take a look at this,' he hissed. 'What did I tell you about them titties?'

'Where? Let me look,' Jeb stage-whispered, trying to push him aside. 'Wowee! Look at that milk-white body all slippery and shiny with soap. Come on, stand up, darlin'.'

'Thass enough. Git outa the way.' Mad Jake heaved him aside and applied his own eye. 'Wow! She's a cowboy's dream come true.'

Sophie was having her back sponged by the maid when she heard some gruff whispering and looked up to see a wild gleaming eye focused on her from a hole in the tent wall. She screamed and snatched for her towel, upsetting the tub and tumbling out.

Mad Jake hooted with laughter and was about to scamper away when he came face to face with one of the Cossacks in his furry hat. The Russian had drawn a short sword from his belt. 'Come on, try me!' Mad Jake snarled and held his scalping knife in readiness. 'I'll cut ya gizzard out.'

The big Cossack's eyes were angrily intense, and he made a quick lunge which Jake parried. The Cossack slashed again and Jake howled as the sword caught his finger, blood splashed and he dropped the knife. The Cossack raised the sword as if to sever Jake's head, but old Jeb shouted out, 'Hold it right there, you varmint.'

Jake stared in dismay at his hand; the top of his third finger was dangling by a thread of skin. 'Look what you've done,' he cried.

'Vot going on here?' Count Alexis appeared, followed by the other Cossack. 'Put that gun away.'

'You tell that critter to back off,' Jeb growled, ''fore I put daylight through his innards.'

The count snapped something in Russian and the Cossack sheathed the sword in the sash of his costume.

Jake sobbed, cursed and shook his hand in pain, at which the finger-top flipped off into the grass. The poodle pounced and golluped it up, licking his snout with satisfaction. 'Now look what you done. I coulda stuck that back on.'

'Zis man's finger must be bandaged up,' the count instructed his butler. 'I zink he vill need ze stitches.'

'I'll do that with pleasure.' The butler smiled, smarmily and led Jake away. 'I'll need two strong men to hold him down.'

'Vy is zis hole in zis tent?'

'Aw, we was only having a bit of fun,' Jeb said, stuffing his revolver back in his belt.

'Vell, you vill have no more such fun on zis expedition or I vill dismiss you all and report you to Captain Hazeltin.'

Jeb shrugged and walked back to the fire. 'I'm gonna enjoy slittin' thet li'l count bastard's throat and pleasurin' his sister, jest you wait and see.'

'Me, I want the maid,' the Swede said. 'I like the dark hair. She a pretty little thing.'

Jeb eyed him severely. 'Don't go goin' soft on her. Remember, they all gotta be killed, the servants, everyone. Dead men tell no tales.'

'*Ja.*' The Swede twitched his pock-holed face. 'I suppose.'

The pine woods along the lakeside resounded with shooting the next day as the count and the princess massacred birds and delicate antelope. They had a close encounter with a large cinnamon bear that came roaring out of the woods and Sophie infuriated him by hitting him in the side with the half-ounce ball of her slim and stylish Pearson sporting rifle. He came on at a run towards them, his fangs bared. The Swede had to step in with his carbine to put him down, pumping all seven shots into the beast.

'Stop it,' Sophie cried. 'You'll ruin the pelt.'

'He would have ruined your pelt if I not.' The Swede stood over the lifeless bear as the black powdersmoke drifted.

Sophie seemed blithely unaware of the danger she might have been in. 'I think I can claim him as mine as I hit him first. He would have died, I'm sure.'

'Don't kid yourself, sister,' Jeb muttered,

and watched greedily as the count took a swig from a silver brandy flask. 'Don't offer us none, your highness, will ya?'

The count ignored him. 'You men, ve vant zis bear transported back to ze camp and skinned. Hurry now, it is getting late.'

Jake was waiting for them when they trailed in, mournfully staring at the throbbing stub of his missing finger. He remembered with a wince how he had blubbered and howled as the butler stuck his needle in, sewing the loose skin together. 'Good job it weren't my trigger finger,' he mused. 'I'm gonna need that when I kill 'em.'

The count and Sophie dressed elegantly for dinner at a trestle table by the lake. The count was in his cream uniform with various sparkling medallions attached to his chest. Sophie wore a high-necked dress of silver satin, with silver bootees. She had her fair hair bundled in a topknot held by the tiara of diamonds. 'This bear steak is really delicious,' she squealed. 'I think I will have him stuffed by a taxidermist. I love being in the Wild West. It is so exciting.'

In the morning, Jake, wrapped in his oversize topcoat and Stetson, told them they would have to move on. 'You've scared all the critters in the neighbourhood away with your shooting. We'll go up Blue Beaver Creek, stay the night at Blue Beaver City, then go look for buffalo.'

'Vot is zat bugling sound I hear in ze mountains?'

'Zat, I mean that, is elk. You gotta use your wits to catch 'em,' Jake said. 'Creep up on 'em downwind; what we call stalking. We ain't got time right now. But, don't worry, there's plenty where we're going.'

'Oh, good.' Sophie clapped her hands with joy. 'That will really be sport. Elk will make a fine trophy.'

'You tell how old they are by how many

tines they got,' the Swede said, entering into the spirit of the thing. He cupped his hands to help her on to her horse. 'May I assist your highness?'

'Poor man,' Sophie said to her maid. 'What on earth has he done to his face? And those awful broken teeth. He seems quite nice underneath. He seems to like you, Marie.'

'Eugh!' Marie brushed the Swede away as he tried to help her into her wagon. 'He is as ugly as sin.'

'Out of the way, my good man.' The butler waggled his fingers, his nose twitching fastidiously at the Swede. 'We can manage without you.'

'It is odd that a cabin in the wilds should cost as much as a room at the Waldorf in New York,' Sophie remonstrated. She might be very rich but she knew the value of a dollar, and Ebediah Pope's prices were somewhat steep.

'That's because there's plenty of rooms

in New York, but there ain't many cabins in these wilds.' Ebediah was adamant. 'That's because folks don't care to live here, or come visiting often. I gotta make my money when I can.'

He had been as surprised as anyone by the arrival of the Russians and had hired them out a cabin at boomtown prices. He had also cooked them a meal of the game they had along, tricked out with fancy doodahs like canned tomatoes, oysters, and stuff that looked like the eggs you would find in a termite mound. They ate it by the bucketful. The roe of some Black Sea fish, apparently. And, as well as champagne and bourbon, they had newfangled cans of lemonade.

When the Russians had retired to their cabins the three hunters sprawled in chairs about Ebediah Pope's fire and got stuck into a barrel of whiskey. 'Seen anything of that stranger we had a li'l argy-bargy with?' Mad Jake enquired innocently, studying his throbbing finger-stub.

'Aincha heard? He got bushwhacked.'

Jeb, huddled in his fur coat, grinned, gummily. 'Oh, yeah? They find out who killed him?'

'He ain't dead.' Ebediah eyed them, suspiciously. 'He near as damn was with a slug in his chest. But it missed his vitals.'

'Ain't dead?' Jeb echoed. 'But he must be. We saw—'

Jake aimed a kick at his shin. 'We saw somebody who said he was dead. If he ain't dead, where is he?'

'Remember that Indian gal you boys raped on my floor here? Waal, you could hardly forget. She's got him.'

'She's got him?' Jake glowered from beneath his stetson and drew his knife, testing its sharpness on his whiskers. 'Whaddaya mean she's got him? Where at?'

'Aw, I don't know,' Ebediah said. 'Ain't no need for you boys to worry about him. He'll be out of action for a good while.'

'You don't know?' Jake leaned over and picked a burning brand from the fire, shoving it within an inch of the whiskey barrel. 'I bet this cabin would sure make a fine blaze. But, mebbe, if Ebediah remembers, that won't happen.'

'Put that back. Don't mess me about.' Ebediah tipped back his derby and wiped sweat from his brow. 'If you really want to know she's probably gotten him hid up at her grandpappy's.'

'An' where's her grandpappy hang out?' Jake still had the burning brand poised over the whiskey barrel. 'You better start talking.'

'Aw, what's it to me? He's one of them shamans. A white-haired galoot. Hangs out in a tipi up along the Wichita Holy Mountain. Reckons it's some kinda staircase to heaven.'

'It surely will be. That Texan on his feet yet?'

'No, I tell ya. He's crocked up. Passing Injin told me the gal's looking after him.'

'It must have been her who took a shot at us,' the Swede said. 'To think she scared us off.'

'It's the last shooting she'll be doing. Jeb, get up there. Finish them.'

'Why me?' Jeb whined.

'Because you're the slipperiest varmint in the Territory. Trickier than a rattler's grandma. Anyway I got more important fish to fry. I gotta attend to these Russians.'

'What do you mean?' Ebediah was startled. 'You're surely not going to—?'

'You can shut your mouth, too. What I mean is I gotta look after them and see to some good hunting. They wanna go looking for buffalo.'

'It ain't wise to go too far out on the plain.'

'No, it ain't, but that's what they want. And they're payin' me a fortune. So thass what they gonna git.'

'What about Comanche?'

'What about 'em? They git killed by

Injins it's their own lookout.'

'Mebbe I oughta warn them.'

'You keep your nose outa our affairs, Mistuh Pope.' Jake tossed the brand back into the fire. 'I ain't warnin' you again. And you, Jeb, you head out for Holy Mountain first light.'

'You're the boss.' Jeb shrugged and looked doleful. 'How about if I take Swede along?'

'You want him to wipe your ass for you? The man's on his back, he can't hurt you. OK, I'll manage on my own. We'll be heading for Jedediah Johnson Lake. Take Swede, and don't make no mistakes.'

Jeb shook his head. 'I coulda sworn we left that fella for buzzard bait.'

'I didn't hear that,' Ebediah said. 'I ain't heard none of your conversation, boys. I'm closing up. Going to bed. Goodnight. You can finish that barrel if you want.'

Mad Jake listened to Ebediah slide the bolt on the door of his sleeping quarters, and padlock it. He eyed the others and made a motion of his thumb across his throat. 'He'll have to go,' he said. 'He knows too much.'

The Swede looked worried. Weren't they, he wondered, biting off more than they could chew?

Eight

One Tooth Jeb and the Swede were given $500 each by Mad Jake as their share of the Texan's cash. McGinty, himself, pocketed $2,000' worth of notes and gold dust. 'I'm the brains of this outfit,' he snarled at them, 'so I get the biggest share.' Not many men cared to argue with Jake when he had that gleam in his eye. And, anyway, $500 was a fortune to the likes of them. There wasn't a lot to spend it on in Blue Beaver City, but Jeb treated himself to a modern miracle, a seven-shot Spencer carbine, like the Swede had. They had been issued to the cavalry towards the end of the war and, with their fast lever action, made the regular muzzle loaders look neanderthal. They bought boxes of .52 bullets for the carbines, loading the slugs into the tubular magazines of the butt-stock. And .45 calibre for their revolvers. 'We gonna make mincemeat of that Texan this time,' Jeb grinned. He bought a bag of bull's-eyes to suck on as he rode along, and they each stuck a bottle of raw whiskey in their belts. They had a day's ride ahead before they reached the sacred mountain.

Princess Sophie watched them go trotting out on their broncs. 'Where are your men going to?' she asked.

'Aw, Jeb's grandmaw got sick an' the Swede's helping him take her a few groceries,' Jake growled. 'They'll catch up in a day or two.'

'What kind men! I do hope they find her well.' Sophie was dressed in a new scarlet riding outfit and fur hat. 'So, today we shoot buffalo?'

'Mebbe today. Mebbe tomorrow. Who knows!'

Jake watched the two burly Cossacks heft from the cabin the small iron safe and place it in the wagon again. Whoo, those boys were strong! 'Ain't goin' nowhere 'til we git paid,' he hooted.

Count Alexis fiddled with the combination as Jake tried to peep over his shoulder like an anxious magpie. He could see the glint of jewellery and silver in there. He felt almost impelled to make his move now, but, no, he'd better bide his time. The count handed him fifteen dollars in notes. 'Five dollar ze day each. Zat is right?'

'It'll do,' Jake muttered as the safe door closed shut. 'Less git this show on the road.'

He strolled back to Ebediah's and bought two small kegs of gunpowder. He put it into gunny sacks and strung it over the Texan's paint horse.

'What you plannin' on doin' with that?' Ebediah shrilled, fearfully.

'Might do a li'l prospectin',' Mad Jake said. He ambled away on his horse, leading the paint, and muttered, 'Them who ask no questions don't git told no lies. It sure should be easy to pop that lil Russian money box.'

Hole-in-the-Shoe had taken to slipping in beside Pete as he lay recuperating from his wound in the buffalo hides. 'I must keep you warm,' she whispered. 'It bad to be cold.' He was in too bad a shape to take much notice of her, except that it was kinda soothing to have a female 'hot water bottle'.

The old grandfather sat smoking his calumet, the peace pipe with its long wooden stem and carved stone bowl, its eagle feathers, each one signifying an enemy touched in battle in times gone by. Some Indian tribes could not afford to lose many warriors so had devised counting coup, a more honourable and less costly form of warfare.

He sat reminiscing about the white man's Big War. 'Your greycoats' rebellion did not do us much good. We only joined because you promised we could keep our slaves and our land after you won. You white people, you always swindle the red man. Your promises were lies. All those who supported the South were turned off their land, if they weren't hunted down and hanged.'

'Yeah, I know.' The former lieutenant stared bitterly at the old man. He knew well enough. Most of his Cherokee friends had gone. 'You musta known the grapes would be sour if we lost. They allus are.'

The old Indian nodded. 'I guess it was not good for you greycoats, either?'

'Serve us right for listenin' to Jeff Davis. What was he? Jest a damn lawyer and politician. He musta known in his heart we couldn't win. The North's got the industrial might.'

Hole-in-the-Shoe, or Spotted Frog, stirred warmly against him, her fingers brushing his abdomen. 'Soon you must try to walk,' she said.

'Yeah,' he grunted. 'I guess so. You

people get on OK with the other tribes in the Territory?'

'Hech!' The old man tossed his white mane. 'There are so many different tribes in the Territory now we have to get along or we would be constantly at war. The army herds in Seminoles from a land called Florida, Apache from Arizona, Delawares, Shawnees, Potawatomis, Kickapoos, and Pawnees from the far north, Choctaws and Chickasaws, even Modocs from a place called California.'

'The Territ'ry's sure become a dumping ground for the tribes.'

'We were told this land was ours in perpetuity. That means for ever. But already the white men have started to carve it up.'

'Trouble is the generation that comes along next has got a different idea of perpetuity than them who made the deal. This is a troublesome, violent country. Even poor ole Abe Lincoln couldn't go to the theatre without gittin' shot. Not that I had much time for him.'

'White man's justice is no justice.'

'Seems to me,' Pete drawled, trying to raise himself, putting an arm around Spotted Frog, 'the only justice a man gets in these parts is his own justice, at the point of a gun.'

'I got a bad feeling,' the old man said, gloomily, passing the pipe across. 'I can sense there will be trouble very soon. Maybe it would be best for you, white man, to go stay with Hole-in-the-Shoe's family in their winter camp. I believe they will have her back.'

Pete hobbled to a sitting position, pulling a buffalo robe around him, and took a puff at the pipe. 'Maybe the gal should go. But I don't know about me. I gotta git on the trail of them lousy rattlesnakes who stole my grubstake. Before they spend it all. Don't suppose you got a spot of whiskey to go with this?'

'No,' the old Indian said. 'I wish I had.' He got up, arthritically, and went to the tipi flap. 'I go pray on the mountain. Maybe that help.'

'Cheerful old buzzard, ain't he?' Pete grinned when he had gone. 'Now less see if you can help me stand up.'

The Swede and old Jeb had made good time and were half-way along the ridge of the Wichitas' sacred mountain before the sun began lowering in the west. Suddenly they heard a strange wailing drifting towards them through the still autumn air and reined in. 'What'n tarnation's that?'

Jeb fumbled for his telescope in the pocket of his tatty fur coat. He peered at a promontory of rock up ahead. 'It's a durn Injin. He's got his arms raised to the sun. It's that ole white hair Ebediah tol' us about.'

'Why he moohahahing like that?'

'Aw, you know the way they go on. See them rock houses built like beehives further up on the ridge? Go on, take a peek. Thass what they call their holy city.

The whole tribe have a big pow wow here at Easter time. Guess he's lookin' after it for 'em. Keepin' the old spirits pacified. Durn fools! Fancy anyone believin' in all that hogwash!'

'Look over there. There's smoke rising out of those trees.'

'Thass where he must have his little hidey-hole. We'll leave the broncs here and go forward on foot. Careful now. They got eyes and ears like hawks, these 'skins.'

They each took a swig of the bottle for Dutch courage and went creeping into a patch of sugar pines. Eventually they reached the edge of a clearing. They peered through sharp-tanged juniper branches and saw one tattered tipi among the usual mess of an Indian encampment. Saplings had been felled for burning and a space cleared. There was a scrubby pony tethered beside a big old grey mare. 'Thass his,' Jeb hissed, thumbing the hammer of the Spencer. Blue smoke was drifting idly from the cone of the tipi. 'Reckon he's in there. I sure am lookin' forward to usin' this on him.'

'Maybe we better wait to sundown,' the Swede said, nervously.

'Yeah, maybe we better had.' Jeb took another gulp from his bottle. 'Then we'll creep in there and blast 'em to bits.'

'We got company.' The grandfather padded into the tipi and sat beside them. 'I can smell them.'

'Who ya seen?'

'I ain't seen nobody. I can smell them over in the woods. An Indian can smell whiskey ten miles away.'

'Mebbe it's them lowdown varmints takin' a second try at me. Pass me my guns.' Pete looked anxiously around. 'Ain't no need for you to git mixed up with this.'

'We already mixed up with you, white man.' The old Wichita grinned across at him and tossed over his gunbelt. 'I pretend not to know them varmints there.

I will go move the horses in case there is shooting.'

'Good thinking. Give me my pants, Frog. I don't wanna die without 'em. It ain't decent.'

The Indian girl rolled out of the buffalo robes and stood in the gloom of the tipi, the flames of the fire slopping shadows over her. She had let her hair down across her cheeks, her eyes lustrous upon him. The bells on her leggings jingled and her firm breasts pressed out the paisley blouse. She pulled on her buckskin skirt to cover her wide belly and stout buttocks. Her teeth flashed a smile at him.

'One way I know I'm sick I never think about sex,' Pete muttered, but he was shot through with a tremor of desire. 'Maybe I'm gittin' healed.'

He thought of the Mexican girl down in Texas who had promised to wait for him. He hadn't seen her since leaving for the war when he was a boy of fifteen. He had written a letter now and again but had not had many replies. Not surprising, as he had been constantly on the move and the postal service wasn't so hot in these parts. Maybe she was already wed. 'Ah, well,' he sighed, 'I already strayed from the primrose path as it is.'

Spotted Frog helped pull his jeans over his long legs. She had mended his canvas shirt and buttoned it on. 'Buckle my gunbelt, Honey. I figure they're waiting for darkness, but we cain't be sure.'

He lay back on the bed and pulled up the base of the tipi skin. 'We gotta sneak outa the back door.'

It was a shock to be out in the dusk, to feel the cold wind cut through him. He shivered violently as Frog wriggled out beside him. 'How do you feel?'

'Not so hot,' he gritted out.

She wrapped a buffalo robe about his shoulders. 'You're not strong enough,' she said.

'I'll be all right. Where you reckon they are?'

She sniffed at the air. 'Down the slope. Over in those junipers.'

'Right, we'll git over behind them logs.' He pointed towards a pile of wood some twenty paces from the tipi door. They crawled across towards them through the long grass. 'Good.' He was breathing hard. 'All we gotta do now is wait.'

Spotted Frog snuggled up beside him. 'Give me one of your revolvers. I can use it.'

Black Pete raised an eyebrow at her. 'Anything you cain't do?' He passed one of his pearl-handled S & Ws across. 'Take care. Double action. Got a hair trigger. Hammer's filed down. Only needs a touch.'

Over in the junipers the two *hombres* watched the old bow-legged Indian shuffling about, hobbling the horses in a new patch of grass. 'He ain't a clue we're here,' Jeb chortled. 'Jest shows how dumb they are.'

116

The dark closed in on them suddenly as the last glimmering rays of the sunset fell away. A silver full moon began to climb over the dark conifers and far off some creature howled, eerily. The eternal struggle of the hunters and the hunted went on. 'Come on.' Jeb took a last slug of the bottle. 'Less go.'

The old Indian had piled their beds with whatever bulky objects he could find so that it would look like they were asleep. He had found his ancient tomahawk with which he had once, many years before, battled with the Osage warriors. And crawled up to join his granddaughter and Black Pete.

'Sure am glad it ain't too cold tonight,' Pete whispered after they had waited some while. 'Hey, hang on. Here they come.'

They watched two shadowy figures creep stealthily forward out of the dark trees through the mist, watched them reach the tipi and, carbines at the ready, push inside. They heard the repeated stuttering blast of explosions, saw the flare of guns through the tipi walls. Pete grinned at her. 'Ready?'

But, as he raised an arm to fire at the two men who came stumbling back out of the tipi, a searing pain jabbed through his half-healed wound. 'Aagh!' Involuntarily he had to pull in his gun hand and the bullet went wild.

Spotted Frog fired, but unused to the lightning-like fingertip touch of the Smith and Wesson, her bullet whined past Jeb's head, making him duck and yell out.

The old Wichita excitedly got to his feet, crying his fate cry, and hurled the tomahawk. But age took its toll on his throw. The weapon merely sliced the Swede's thigh and he squealed and hopped in agony. Jeb's carbine barked out and the Indian hurtled backwards, a slug in his chest.

Pete and Spotted Frog fired again, but by this time the two men had their heads down and were dodging back into the darkness of the trees.

'Hot damn! They tricked us,' the Swede groaned.

Jeb pumped his carbine but his seven had gone. He cursed and pulled his revolver, blazing away at whoever was behind the pile of logs.

The Swede went hobbling away, hanging on to his injured leg. As lead spat and ricocheted about him Jeb, too, turned tail and ran off through the pines.

When they reached the broncs the Swede was whining about the bloody gash in his thigh. 'I gonna bleed to death.'

'Ah, shuddup.' Jed hoisted him on to his horse. 'We gotta git outa here. That man's got eyes in the back of his head.'

Spotted Frog ran after them and heard the thud of hooves as they high-tailed it back down the mountainside. 'Come back you yellow cowards.' She blasted wildly away with the .32 after them until the cylinder was empty. 'I will kill you.'

Pete wasn't up to walking far or giving chase. He knelt down beside the old

Wichita who was staring at the rising moon. His fore-sense of danger had proved true. 'He's going,' he said, as the girl returned to stand beside him. 'Going to the green valley, pastures new.'

Spotted Frog knelt down beside him. There were large tears rolling down her dark face, splashing on to the old man.

The Wichita gave a gasp of pain and looked at her. 'Your tears are my tears,' he said. 'Say farewell to the family for me. Tell them I say you a good girl. Tell them I died well.'

'You die like a warrior,' she said, through her tears.

The old man nodded, and turned to Pete. 'My granddaughter, look after her for me, white man.'

Pete wasn't sure what to say to that. It sounded a tad like emotional blackmail. 'She'll be OK. So will you.' He gripped the old man's hands as he closed his eyes. There was a rattling sound in his throat, and he was gone.

'Grandfather,' she cried, hugging him. 'Why did you have to be such a fool jumping up like that? Now I will miss you. It is not good to be alone.'

Pete raised her up, putting an arm around her. 'C'mon inside,' he said. 'He'll be all right here tonight. Tomorrow we'll take him up to your holy city. See him on his way. He sure was a brave ole warrior. That's what he was.'

'They got away,' she said, as they went back to the tipi. 'Promise me, Pete, you will kill them. You will avenge grandfather.'

'Waal,' he groaned, sinking back on to the buffalo-skin couch. 'I kin try. It ain' vengeance I want, it's my durn cash. One thang's fer sure, I don't reckon they'll be back tonight.'

Nine

'Look, surely those are buffalo tracks!' Sophie cried out with delight as, sitting side-saddle in her long skirt, she rode her horse over to examine a wide swathe of cloven-hooved marks and heavy droppings heading away over the plain.

'Naw! You plumb crazy?' Mad Jake gave a hoot of derision. 'Them's cows.'

'Cows?' the count echoed, as he sat his long-legged English thoroughbred. Are you sure?'

'You furriners ain' got no idea. 'Course them's cows. There's thousands of wild longhorns bin left to roam wild down in Texas while the war raged. Men are herdin' 'em up to the northern markets. Even up as far as Wyoming, so I hear. These musta come up the trail blazed by Jess Chisholm.'

'These don't look like cows to me,' Sophie said, eyeing the backwoodsman curiously. 'But I guess you know best.'

'Sure I do, li'l lady.' Jake spat a gob of baccy and grinned at her. 'I've tol' ya, you want buff' you got to go out on to the plain, thisaway.'

'I vould love to bag a buffalo in the Vild Vest to say I had done so.'

'Well,' Sophie smiled at her brother. 'We won't be here again, will we? So let's try.'

They spent the night on the shore of Jedediah Johnson Lake and decimated some more duck. They were somewhat pestered by flies because of all the raw heads and hides they were carrying as souvenirs, but they had taken the precaution of bringing mosquito nets. They were doing so much shooting McGinty had to go back to Blue Beaver City to stock up on bullets for their rifles. Or so he said. Sophie suspected it more likely he had run out of whiskey. Those three seemed to be forever drunk. When he returned, sure enough, she could smell it on his breath. She gave an involuntary shudder whenever he came near, such a crass, uncouth creature with his horrible little bloodshot eyes forever boring into her, his awful unwashed smell. But she had to admit he was a good hunter. He led them on to a string of lakes teeming with trout. They saw otters and more beaver but they gave them a truce. It was elk they were interested in now.

When they reached the southern end of the long and placid Frenchman's Lake she had been excited to hear their bugling up in the woods. McGinty gave them the nod and led them up through the trees. 'I should think the elk could smell him coming,' she whispered to her brother.

'No, ve are down vind. It is ve who smell him.'

But, there the elk was, his great head of antlers silhouetted against the setting sun. Thrilled by the sight, Sophie aimed as instructed below his foreleg, but it was probably McGinty's shot brought him down. She couldn't be sure. He fired immediately after her as the rest of the herd went racing away.

Before dinner Count Alexis, himself an expert taxidermist, was already busy with his bottles of chemicals preserving the head. He stroked the numerous tines of the antlers and called out, 'Zis must have been an old varrior.'

Sophie smiled as she bathed and dressed for dinner in her tent. She could hear the butler laying out the silver on a trestle table by the shore of the lake and McGinty shouting some insult at him in his drunken way. 'How exciting it is out here,' she said to her maid. 'I never want to go back home.'

Each night she had gone to sleep with thoughts of the handsome American captain in her head. Franklin had said he would see them in seven days. Already nine had passed and she crossed them from her calendar, impatiently. Her heart pounded, breathlessly, as she remembered how he had touched her knee beneath the dinner table, and boldly kissed her hand when they parted. Did she dare go any further? She felt like a bird released from her cage, she was free, she could dare anything in this lovely country. She was blindly oblivious to McGinty, the bedraggled hawk waiting to pounce.

As if in answer to her dreams the next morning she heard a haloo on a bugle and saw a company of blue-bellies kicking up dust as they cantered across the plain, the standard of the Tenth Company US Cavalry rippling in the breeze. And there at the head of them was Captain Hazeltin. He sprang from his white charger and ran towards her. Sophie thought he was going to sweep her up into his arms. But he came to a halt, clicked his spurred boot-heels and gave a flourishing salute. 'Your Highness, it is so good to see you again.'

'And you, Franklin.' She proferred her

hand and he raised it to his lips. 'You are just in time for some morning tea.'

The captain gave the order to his sergeant for his troopers to make camp and to take it easy. The all-blacks gave wide, arrogant grins as they watched him go into the princess's tent.

'They've got tight-curled hair like buffalo hide,' Sophie said.

'That's probably why the Indians call them buffalo soldiers,' the captain replied, shaking hands with the count, who was still at breakfast.

'Help yourself, old chap. Vot vould you like? Trout, pickled eggs, or ze elk steaks?'

'Don't mind if I do. A nice trout would be fine. We've ridden a long way looking for you. How's the hunting, sir?'

'Excellent. Ve are very pleased.'

'No trouble with your guides?'

'No, no trouble. Ze ozzer two haf gone somevere but zey will catch up.'

'They are very insolent,' Sophie said. 'In

Russia I would have had them flogged, but I do not believe that is possible here. Any serf of ours has to leave the room backwards, head bowed, if he does not want a flogging.'

'No, I'm afraid the war abolished all that sort of thing. How many serfs have you?'

'About four hundred on our country estate. They are not really the same as what you would call slaves. They are part of our estate. They depend on us. There is foolish talk of emancipation in Russia, too. But what would they do? Where would they go?'

'I really don't know. I suppose they could join the army. All my chaps were slaves at one time.'

'Zat is different,' the count snapped, as the butler poured tea from a silver samovar. 'Zey are Negroes. Our peasants, zey are lower zan animals.'

'Really?' Franklin picked at his trout and creamed potatoes. 'We here have a very democratic country.'

'Everybody is free,' Sophie smiled. 'Except your Indians.'

'Well, no, they just don't see eye to eye with us. They have to be constrained. And, speaking of that, I have what may be some bad news for you—and for the Indians. My regiment is being sent south to Arizona. Custer's Seventh is taking over.'

'Custer? General Custer? Oh, I would love to meet him.'

'He is not actually a general now. He was brevet general in the war. Now he is a colonel. He is married, actually, and he always brings his wife along with him.'

'Really?' Sophie giggled. 'Isn't she lucky.'

'Lucky or not, *I* do not feel lucky,' the captain murmured. 'This is probably the last time I will be able to see you, Princess.'

Franklin stared at her with his dark and soulful eyes, his black wiry goatée jutting, his neatly brushed hair hanging long, swept back over his collar. Sophie thought how dashing he looked in his uniform. She put out her hand to touch him. 'I am sorry to hear that, Captain.'

'Sir, may I beg a favour? May I monopolize your sister's company today? I would like to go riding with her?'

'Riding?' The count was busy having his whiskers clipped by the butler. 'Sure. Vy not? I am getting tired of the hunt. I vill take it easy, as you say. Be sure to have her back by nightfall. Do you need one of my Cossacks?'

'No,' the captain added hastily. 'She will be perfectly safe with me. That is if she is willing to trust me.'

'Of course I am,' Sophie laughed. 'We can have a picnic, explore the lakes. We do not need any servants, Alexis. All that stuffiness. I want to ride free with the captain.'

The count eyed her for moments, a flicker of concern in his eyes. 'Just you be careful, yes?' He flicked his fingers, dismissing them. 'Go along.'

Black Pete buckled on his twin .32s, checked his Winchester was fully primed. The Wichita girl helped him on with his grey greatcoat. 'You feel OK?'

'Sure,' he whispered, waving her away as he went to get on his grey mare. He groaned as he hauled himself up into the saddle. 'I feel a lot better now, thanks to you.' He pulled his hat firm, tightened the reins. 'Let's go get 'em.'

The Indian girl jogged off behind him on her grandfather's pony, holding the long-barrelled buffalo gun in her hand.

They made good time to Blue Beaver City. There were a couple of trappers around loading up their furs, and Ebediah was coming out of the livery where he had been shoeing a horse. 'Hi,' he called, seemingly surprised to see them. 'So you're still alive.'

'We sure are,' the Texan said. 'Them varmints ain't put us down yet.'

'Come on in and have a drink and a bite to eat.' It was nearly dusk and the trading store was a welcome sight, blue smoke rising from its chimney stack.

Ebediah led them towards the verandah steps when suddenly there was a loud explosion and the cabin erupted in flames. The blast hurled them off their feet and they were showered with burning debris which was scattered fifty feet in the air.

'What in tarnation?' Ebediah yelled, as he hoisted a log plank off himself and got to his feet. 'What ... how ...?'

'You OK?' Pete helped the girl up and brushed some cinders from her.

They all gawped at the demolished cabin which was blazing merrily. All that was left in the centre was the blackened iron stove. 'I've a feelin' you shoulda been in there.'

'Me?' Mr Pope gaped. 'Why?'

'Because you know too much about certain parties.'

'But how? Mad Jake cain't have done it. He's been out three days with them Russkies.'

'What Russkies?'

'Aw, some crazy count and his princess sister. They're spending money like there's no tomorrow. Mad Jake and them other two's led 'em out on a huntin' party to shoot elk and buffalo.'

The other trappers had run up to stare at the burning timbers and to ask what had happened. 'Somebody drop a match on a keg of powder or somethun'?' one asked.

'Nope. This weren't no accident.' As the flames began to die down the Texan took a stick and began to rake through the intense heat of the embers. His hunch proved right. He flicked out some wires attached to which were the remains of a tin alarm clock. 'You see this? You know whose work this is?'

'No.'

'Mad Jake's. I'd bet my bottom dollar. He's an expert with bombs. Learned it in the war. My guess is he came sneaking back here in the night and attached a twenty-four hour device to a barrel of gun-powder. He probably concealed it in

Ebediah's woodshed and when the time ticked out: boom!'

'How would that be possible?'

'Anythang's possible. They got underwater torpedoes, all sorts of gadgets these days. He may be crazy but he's a genius when it comes to explosives. I've watched him.'

'The dirty lowdown skunk. He coulda killed me, killed us all. That's my livelihood gone up.'

'Yeah, we were lucky. One step closer—powee!'

'Why should he want to kill Ebediah?'

'Because he knows they tried to kill me. Mad Jake don't believe in leaving anyone to tell the tale.'

'So, he thought iffen he's out hunting with that count nobody could link him with this.'

'You got it,' the Texan said. 'What worries me is what's gonna happen to this count and this princess. Were they carrying any valuables?'

'They had a whole damn safe full. You shoulda seen them rubies round that gal's throat.'

'Jeez,' the Texan breathed out. 'They ain't gonna be round that throat for long with them three murderous bustards along. We gotta go after 'em. And as fast as we can.'

'First we'll put a meal inside you and bed you down in one of these other cabins.'

'Yeah, we'll move out first light.'

'You put a slug in that mad dog, mistuh, for me,' Pope said.

'I'll try,' Pete grinned. 'It's gotten kinda personal now. Them madmen will stop at nuthin'.'

Ten

Captain Hazeltin had got that dopey look on his face. He was in love. He felt like he was floating on cottonwool clouds way above ordinary mortals. He smiled at everybody. He wanted them to share his happiness. He was, after all, only twenty-four, and had never been so smitten. He felt like his heart was bursting, that he could not bear to be apart from his princess. They rode together through the solid granite Wichita Mountains, which stood like sentinels above the great plains hundreds of feet below. They followed the shores of the lakes, and ventured into a red sandstone canyon, where luxuriant trees were fed by a clear spring. They marvelled at the profusion of wildlife, agile otters, mischievous raccoons, brilliantly coloured snakes, a spiky porcupine climbing into a tree, hundreds of different birds, sapsuckers and nuthatches, and others they could not identify. They did not shoot at anything. There was a serene, spiritual quality about these canyons and mountains that they did not want to desecrate. Sophie was surprised at herself for she loved to hunt. But for once she was content to watch and wonder for her heart, too, was pounding with excitement at being alone in this wilderness beside her handsome captain. They picnicked by a pool where there were tracks of elk and deer. They cooled a bottle of wine in the water and lay beside each other, tantalizingly almost touching. Maybe it was the thought they had so little time, maybe it was the heady effect of the wine but, suddenly, they had rolled together into each other's arms and were kissing and breathing deep, and kissing some more like they were the only two people whose lips had ever met. They were late back that night and Princess

Sophie looked tousled and windswept, but elated, too.

'I have decided to stay on for two days and enjoy a little hunting with our Russian guests,' Captain Hazeltin told First Lieutenant Clay.

'Huntin'?' Clay grinned. 'Is that what you call it? Me, I'd use another word.'

The captain flushed scarlet. 'That's enough of your insolence. You can tell the men they can enjoy some more rest and recreation. They've no objection to that, have they?'

'No, suh. You enjoy yourself, suh, with that li'l princess. Don't you worry none about us. We ain' got no gals, but—'

'That will be all, Clay,' Hazeltin snapped, shaving his side-cheeks to his goatee, sprucing himself up to go dine with the count and Sophie. 'We will return to the fort in two days to make ready to hand over to Custer.'

The next day Sophie and the captain went out riding again, searching for a secluded spot in the woods. The men enjoyed their rest, lazing around the shore of the lake, fishing, wrestling, hunting, racing their horses, playing cards and dice, or just sitting around chatting, whatever they cared to do. There were many ribald remarks about what their captain was up to. In the evening they cooked fresh trout and haunches of antelope over their fires and Captain Hazeltin and Sophie could hear them having a sing-song, their deep bass voices in rhythmic harmony, led by the tremulous tenor of one of the boys, accompanied by flute, drum and mouth organ. Sophie shivered and reached for the captain's hand. 'It is beautiful,' she whispered.

Mad Jake's two cronies, Jeb and the Swede, had by this time returned from visiting 'granny' with the news that they had 'taken care of things'. They didn't dare tell him that the Texan was still alive. They were worried by the presence of the soldiers, the delay, impatient to carry out their plan and move on out.

'When we gonna do it?' the Swede hissed, examining the axe cut in his leg. There was a nasty green pus beneath the dirty bandage.

'I sure weren't 'spectin' thet dum smartypants captain to be hanging around,' Jake told them. 'This puts a different 'plexion on things.'

'Whassit matter,' old Jeb whispered. 'Let's lead 'em out on to the plains. Stick to our plan. Say the Comanch' kilt 'em, if anybody ever catches up. Comanch' jest as likely to kill a captain as a count. They ain' fussy.'

Jake spat a gob of baccy juice at the passing butler. 'That figgers. I'll try an' persuade the count to move out on to the plain if he wants buff'lo. If that captain wants to come sniffing after her skirts he can come, too.'

The Swede peered back over his shoulder the way they had come, half-expecting to see the avenging Texan. 'We make our move soon?'

'Sure, what you frettin' at?' Jake then shouted at the Cossacks, 'Hey, you two fat apes, start loadin' up your gear. We're gonna be movin' outa here. Don't just stand there.'

One of the Cossacks frowned at him and snarled, *'Yob tvoyu mat!'* (which wasn't a nice thing to say about Mad Jake's mother).

'Lookee here, Count,' Mad Jake told him. 'You ain' gonna find any buff'lo round here. You want any we gonna have to move along to the ridge of the mountains then we can ride down on to the plain.'

The count frowned, but agreed, and gave orders to move out. To Jake's chagrin Captain Hazeltin said he would ride along with them for another day. 'We better wait 'til he's gawn,' he told his boys. 'Then we'll do it.'

The column of tarpaulin-covered wagons

set off through the mountains as the three guides rode forward to blaze a path. 'I feel like a homesteader heading out west to find a new home,' Sophie exclaimed. 'Wouldn't it be wonderful, Franklin, if we could just go on and on, put down roots in Oregon or California? They say it's paradise out there, peaches grow as big as melons. We could have our own ranch.'

'A wonderful dream,' the captain said, reaching across to squeeze her hand. 'But, alas, it cannot be. I'm a twenty-year man.'

'Couldn't you just desert? We could change our names, disappear.'

'Princess!' The captain was shocked. 'Desert? I couldn't do that. I am a gentleman. Think of my family, my friends.'

'Oh, foo! Do you put silly honour before being with me?'

'What about you? You have to return to Russia. There would be a scandal, an outcry. There would be no hiding place.'

'Ach!' she exclaimed. 'I am not so important. There are hundreds of princesses in Russia. I am a modern girl. I do not want to go back to that melancholy country. I know! We could pretend we were captured by Indians. It is easy to disappear.'

'I only wish we could,' he muttered. 'The thought of parting from you tears me apart.'

That night they reached a place called Sunset Pool. After dinner they stole away and, lying in each other's arms, watched the pool turn to molten gold as the sun lowered. They saw a herd of deer come timorously down to the pool through the dusk to drink and Captain Hazeltin whispered, 'Sophie, I have wronged you. I should not have come.'

'Don't be silly,' she said, stroking his beard and toying with his gilt buttons. 'It has been wonderful.'

'Sophie, will you marry me?'

'Marry you?'

'I know it sounds absurd, the difference in our social standing, you a princess but, a captain's salary, I know it's only a hundred dollars a month, but it is not to be sneezed at and, with my small private income, I couldn't keep you as you are accustomed, grand palaces and all that, but we could be comfortable, we could be happy.'

'A hundred dollars a month!'

'Don't say it like that! You make me feel wretched. Pretend I never asked. I'm such a fool. How could I expect you to follow me to Arizona, to live in some dusty fort in the desert surrounded by hostile Apaches? It would be no life for you, my dear.'

'It sounds wonderful! Of course I'll marry you, my darling.'

'You will?' he shouted, doubtfully. 'You mean you will?'

'Of course, I will,' she smiled, pulling him down upon her. 'As soon as we can. I can't wait to be your wife.'

The captain sang to himself, his heart full of joy, as he prepared to ride away the next morning. The count had given his consent to their marriage, with some reluctance, it had to be admitted. It was agreed that Sophie and the captain would announce their betrothal when the princess and count returned to Fort Sill from their hunting trip.

The black boys were waiting for him, lined up on their horses for inspection. They sat their mounts with a careless ease, their campaign hats pulled over their brows in rakish fashion, their fine physiques in their tight pants and cavalry jackets, relaxed and arrogant.

'From that smile on the Cap's face it looks like antelope ain' all he's bin pumpin' his bullets into,' one grinned, causing a ripple of laughter through the ranks.

'Shut up,' the black sergeant growled.

The captain blushed. 'I think it is permissible for me to tell you men that the princess has consented to accept my hand in marriage.'

Shrill wolf-whistles and cheers greeted this news. Orders were shouted out and the platoon wheeled away back towards Fort Sill, Captain Hazeltin riding proudly at their head, the regimental flag rippling in the breeze, as Sophie waved farewell.

Eleven

Black Pete and Spotted Frog were crossing the plain heading towards Frenchman's Lake when the Indian girl scented the air, slid from her piebald pony and put an ear to the ground. 'Horsemen coming,' she cried in her own language. 'Many of them.'

Pete looked around for cover, but there were no rocks nearby. He followed his instinct from the years of guerrilla fighting, jumped from his mare and pulled the horse down into the long dry grass. He lay on her neck, holding his hand over her nose, soothing her. Spotted Frog did the same with her well-schooled pony. They watched through the grass and saw a column of cavalry go thundering past at a fast lope.

'Buffalo soldiers,' the girl hissed. 'Such

men were once our slaves. Now they ride through our land.'

'Blue-bellies,' Pete growled, the bitterness of the war returning to him. 'I'd jest as soon not have a run-in with 'em.'

They jogged on their way at a steady lope until they reached the lake. 'My family are in winter camp to the north of here,' she said, pointing. Pete had his wound tight-bound with rawhide and although it still pained him it was staying closed. They came to a camping ground where fires had been lit, obviously the cavalry, and further along flattened grass where tents had been pitched, and there were wine and champagne bottles scattered about. 'Sure looks like somebody's been havin' a party.'

They followed the indentations of wagon wheels and, as they passed through a grove of aspens quivering in the breeze, they came face to face with a bearded man in a fur hat and buckskins leading a mule loaded with dead critters.

Pete's hand went to his revolver ready to draw until he saw that the fellow was an old trapper. 'Howdy,' he called. 'Seen any sign of three varmints name of Jake, Jeb and Swede?'

The trapper had a long-barrelled musket in his hand and he eyed the Texan's rebel-grey frock coat with apprehension. 'Mebbe I have.'

'Wadda ya mean mebbe you have? You either have or you haven't.'

'What's your business with 'em, mistuh?'

'Them three lousy polecats bushwhacked me, stole my paint hoss and my cash, that's what.'

'They sure as dang looked a scurvy-faced bunch. Bumped into 'em a way back. They're actin' as guides to the count.'

'So we heard.'

'That princess is the sassiest li'l bitch as I seen in a month of Sundays. Drinkin' and larkin' about in the woods she was.'

'That explains the champagne trail.'

'Yep. Them folks sure like to enjoy

'emselves. She had a captain of cavalry along.'

'A captain? What's he doing?'

'What comes natural. I seen him and the princess philly-anderin' in the woods. The boy's sure got the hots for her.'

'Philly-anderin'?' Spotted Frog echoed. 'What is this?'

'Means she's on heat,' Pete said, tipping back his hat to hang on his shoulders by its cord, and pushing fingers through his dusty black hair. 'How far they ahead?'

The leathery old trapper shrugged. 'Day's ride. They were up along by the Sunset Pool when I seen 'em. I ain't needed to do much hunting. I been skinnin' all the critters they shot. I'm going into Blue Beaver City.'

'Yeah? Somebody's blown up the trading store. Ebediah had a lucky escape. I reckon it was Mad Jake.'

'How could Mad Jake do it when he's with them blue-bloods?'

'He's got ways. Where you reckon them

varmints are takin' 'em?'

'They were headin' on under the Big Mountain, the trail leads down on to the plains. They reckoned they wanted to shoot buffalo.'

'Comanche country.' Spotted Frog's dark eyes were troubled. 'Red Bone's country. He has been raiding and burning. Bad medicine. White man think all Indians bad like him.'

'Yeah, we better git after 'em. So long, mistuh.'

'So long,' the trapper called. 'Good huntin'.'

'Now we got rid of that captain we're in business, boys.'

Mad Jake, wrapped in his oversize overcoat, had rolled out of his blanket from beneath one of the wagons. He scratched himself, hungover and ornery from the effects of too much red-eye the night before. He joined the others around the campfire, poured himself thick black coffee from a tin jug and tipped in the last of the bottle as hair of the dog. His throbbing finger stub made him feel mean as a buckshot grizzly. The Swede's festering leg and broken teeth, and Jeb's sore head, had a similar effect on them.

'Get your guns ready, boys,' Jake growled.

He ambled over to the tent where the count and Sophie were sitting outside tinkling teacups and being served breakfast by the pudgy butler in his velveteen suit. 'You wanna shoot buff'lo you gonna have to go down on to the plains through thet gap,' Jake said.

They had reached the rim of the granite ridge and the sunbleached plains stretched out below them. The count took his time answering. 'I don't think ve vill bother. Ve haff things to arrange back at ze fort, eh, Sophie? Ve haff had enough of hunting. You men vill guide us back.'

'Ve vill, vill ve?' Jake grinned.

The tall Cossack was standing behind

the count, his arms folded, on duty as usual. His fatter friend was away by the cook's fire washing his bald head in a canvas bowl. The tall one watched Jake through narrowed eyes.

'They're plannin' on going back,' Jake told his boys. 'You ready? It's time we took 'em. Don't touch the princess. That purty li'l thang is gonna be mine.'

'Dirty bitch,' Jeb snarled. 'Sittin' there all spruced up an' polite-talkin'. You'd think butter wouldn't melt in her mouth. I know what she's been up to with that captain.'

'She'll git what she deserves. Once, I'm done with her she gits her throat slit.'

'Yeah?' The Swede looked alarmed, but limped over to pull his Spencer carbine from his saddle boot. He snapped a round into the breech. 'I take the fat Cossack.'

'The li'l butler's mine,' Jeb giggled. 'I'm gonna smack his ass. The rest's a piece of cake.'

'I'll put air through the tall Cossack,'

153

Jake snarled. 'They all gotta go down.'

'Not Marie,' the Swede said. 'I take her with me as my woman.'

'He's gawn soft in the brain.' Jake winked at Jeb, and looked around. There wasn't another soul in sight on the high ridge or across the wide plains of buffalo grass. He pulled his revolver from the thick leather belt around his shabby overcoat, cocked it, and nodded at the Swede. 'Go git him.'

The Cossack was still splashing and spluttering over the canvas bowl, flipping water over his bare body and armpits. The Swede went up behind him and muttered, gutturally, 'I sure sorry 'bout this, Russkie.' The Cossack froze as the cold barrel pressed into his back. The Swede squeezed the trigger and blasted a hole in his spine. The Russian went jerking and crashing to the ground.

'What on earth?' The butler was in the act of serving cranberry sauce from a silver salver. He jumped so with fright it went all over the count's waistcoat front. The tall Cossack behind his master whipped out his broad sword from his sash and charged towards the gunmen. But it was too late. Jake's revolver crashed out and he rolled over like a jack-rabbit, hitting the dust. The Swede levered his carbine pumping bullets into him until he had stopped twitching.

Jeb aimed his carbine at the count, the shot scattering breakfast dishes. But the count didn't wait to be shot at. As Sophie screamed he dodged from the table and raced for his thoroughbred, which was saddled in readiness for him. He leaped on to it, scrambled feet into stirrups and shouted, *'Run,* Sophie!'

Jake ran to grab her by her fair hair as she tried to escape. 'Stop him!' he shouted, firing his revolver at the count. 'He's gittin' away.'

He threw the screaming and scratching Sophie down into the dust, trying to secure her, as the Swede and Jeb aimed their carbines at the fleeing count. Several bullets whistled past the royal head, but soon the thoroughbred had galloped with him swiftly beyond their range.

'Aw, hell,' Jeb moaned. 'I coulda hit him first time but I'se worried I mighta kilt thet bitch.'

The princess was using very unladylike language as Jake tried to restrain her.

As the count went streaking away across the grass towards the shelter of the woods his three black-clothed manservants went running after their master. The Swede took them down, potting them like game, and one by one they crumpled into the grass.

The paunchy butler, his face puckered and trembling with fear, tripped over a chair as he tried to back away. 'Come here, you li'l pink piggy.' Jeb jumped on him, pulling his velvet pantaloons down, smacking his backside, whooping with glee as he rode him.

Marie was watching with horror, her mouth open. 'All right,' the Swede said, catching hold of her around the waist. 'We no kill you. You gonna be mine.' Marie started screaming as he hoisted her bodily up into the back of a wagon and scrambled in on top of her. 'Shuddup. Don't worry,' he shouted, scrabbling at her skirts. 'You gonna be my missus.'

'That yeller-belly count sure didn't wait for you, sister,' Jake gasped out, as he wrestled with Sophie on the ground. She was biting, cursing, kicking like a wildcat. His words were drowned by the shrill screams of Marie and the butler.

After a while it went quiet. Jeb wiped blood from his knife on the sleeve of his filthy fur coat and grinned down at the prostrate, pink-haunched butler. 'Thet settled the li'l pig. It sure felt good to slice his gizzard.'

The Swede jumped down from the wagon doing up his buttons and a grin cracked his pockmarked face. They could hear Marie sobbing inside. 'She soon get to like me. We get married. I tell her.'

Mad Jake had finally got a rope around Sophie's wrists and bound her arms tight. 'The li'l hellcat,' he muttered. 'I'll deal with her later. First things first. Let's take a look at that safe.'

He got up, stuffing his revolver back into his belt, kicking out at one of the Cossacks on the ground. 'Damn fat bastard. You ain't so handy with your knife now. You two, git thet safe outa the wagon.'

When they had manhandled it to the ground Jake examined the lock, fiddling the controls to no effect. 'Go git me the barrel of gunpowder,' he muttered, and began work with the dedication of an expert. He poured gunpowder through grass straws into the hinges and sprinkled it liberally beneath the safe.

'Iffen you two don't wanna lose your eyebrows you better step back.' Jake grinned and sat cross-legged perched on top of the safe. He carelessly struck a match and lit fuses as the Swede and Jeb scrambled away.

Whooompf! The explosion numbed their ears. As a black cloud of smoke cleared they saw that the safe door had swung open and Mad Jake was still sitting upon it intact.

'The secret is I'm so close to the explosion it don't bother me none,' he said, kneeling down to take the contents from the safe. 'Whoowhee! Look at this. A treasure trove.'

He stuck in his hand and pulled out Sophie's jewellery as she watched, her eyes glimmering fiercely, trussed like a chicken by the tight rope. Jake held up with delight her diamond-encrusted diadem, her ruby necklace, bracelets, brooches, gold rings with emerald stones, ear bobs, the count's silver cufflinks and studs, cigar case, and medallions adorned with precious gems. That was apart from the wads of greenbacks and silver coin.

The Swede pinned a glittering star-shaped medal on his chest. 'How you like?' he said proudly to Marie as she clambered from the wagon tugging up her drawers. Her hair was down over her eyes and she looked around with dismay at the bodies and wreckage.

'Toss that in the sack,' Jake ordered. 'We'll have a share-out when we git over the border.'

'Yee-hoo!' Jeb hollered, waving his hat in the air. 'We done it. I'm gonna git me a new set of teeth and open a saloon.'

'Me an' Marie, we're goin' to Mexico.'

'Aw, shuddup. We got to get away from here first.'

Pete and Frog reined in their mounts as they heard an explosion and saw a cloud of black smoke billow into the air. They had ridden through the night. 'That's about two miles away,' he said. 'Looks like we might be too late.'

Normally, he would have spurred his mare on at a gallop, but he was afraid of opening the wound in his chest and, anyhow, she was plumb tuckered out.

They pushed on at a trot and suddenly saw a man in a cream-coloured uniform, hatless, riding hard towards them. When he saw them he hauled the glistening chestnut in, as if to veer away. His blue eyes were startled. Perhaps he thought they were part of the gang. Pete raised his gloved hand in salute and hollered out, 'We're friends.' The count trotted warily towards them. He pointed back. 'Zis is terrible,' he screeched. 'Zey are killing everyone.'

'Yeah,' Pete muttered darkly. 'Pity I didn't git here an hour earlier. I coulda saved you a heap of trouble.'

'You know zose men?'

'Yeah, we've met before. Murderin' scum. You shoulda never hired 'em.'

He figured the dainty little rider with the pointed blond beard must be the count he'd heard about. 'All we can do is git after 'em, pronto.'

They rode to the scene of the massacre, looked at the bodies in the grass who stared up with lifeless eyes at the blue cloudless sky. 'One thang's for sure,' Pete muttered. 'The buzzards are gonna have a good feed.' They were already circling up above.

'My poor sister. They must have taken her with them. And her Russian maid.'

'Waal, you can guess what they're plannin' for them.'

'Oh, God!' the count sobbed. 'If only I had had my gun at hand I could have fought them.'

'Yep?' Pete made a wry grimace. He stood on the rim, the prairie wind rippling his shirt. 'I reckon they gone down through Burford Gap. If we wanna git them back we got no time to lose.'

'They've stolen all our valuables, too. I—I—I'd better go back,' the count stuttered. 'I'll raise the soldiers at the fort.'

Pete studied him. The little creep's in a funk, he thought. 'Waal, you probably wouldn't be no use to me. All your kind's good for is killin' dumb animals.'

'The soldiers will know what to do.'

'By then it'll be too late. But go on, you go back. Your trail of bottles and blood'll show you the way.'

'Aren't you going to bury my people?'

'Mistuh, you can if you want. I ain't got the time or inclination for buryin'.' He swung up on the grey and kneed her forward. 'Come on, Frog.'

Mad Jake had made camp in a hollow of the prairie. Night was coming on, dark thunderclouds rumbling up ahead, and he was anxious to examine their loot and have his way with Sophie before it rained. He hunkered down to make a small fire of buffalo chips, blowing at it vigorously. 'We gotta git a helluva long way away from this Territ'ry. Now you let the count go everybody gonna know what we done.'

'How could we stop him?' old Jeb whined. 'He went as fast as a rat outa his bolthole. He sure didn't hang about to save his little sister.'

'Waal, I guess he's got the right idea, ain't he? Look after number one. Save your own hide.'

'They will hunt you all down,' Sophie hissed, squatting in her bonds a little distance away. 'They won't rest until they have caught you.'

'Thass so?' Jake squinted up at her through his red-rimmed eyes, and paused from flapping at the fire with his hat. 'In that case we better enjoy ourselves while we can.'

He strode over to her, caught her by her hair and pulled her to her knees so that she was kneeling in front of him. 'Now, your highness—' He pulled out his revolver, cocked it, and held it to her temple. 'I bet you weren't so reluctant about pleasurin' the captain.'

'Please, don't kill me,' the crouching girl whimpered as he stood over her. 'I'll do anything you want. Please!'

'Good,' Jake grunted. 'Thass my girl.'

The Swede stood up to get flour from his saddle-bag. He made a croaking screech. 'Aach!'

'What's the matter now?' Mad Jake looked round and saw that a feathered arrow had gone clean through the Swede's neck. It was flint-tipped with partridge-feather flights. 'Shee-it,' he cried, pulling away from the girl, brandishing his revolver, firing at one of the Comanche and diving into the grass as another arrow hissed past his head.

Jeb snatched up his carbine, crouching up, snapping off a shot, cutting one of the Comanche down. There were seven of them, a small war party, near-naked, dark copper-coloured, their faces and bodies daubed with paint, come out of nowhere. He levered the carbine and stood his ground as they dashed forward. Kapow! The carbine cracked out spinning a second one to the ground. Jeb pumped another slug into the breech, but with a howl of anger a Comanche had leaped upon him.

Jeb stared up in terror at the savage face, the feathers dangling from a scalp-lock. A tomahawk flashed and the old man screamed as what remained of his hair was ripped away.

Mad Jake shuddered when he heard the scream. He wriggled away through the long grass as fast as he could go. Fortunately, the air had become dark as the thundercloud rolled up over them and lightning streaked its daggers across the sky. It distracted the Comanche and covered Jake's tracks. He peered up out of the grass. The Texan's paint horse was grazing close by where he had been hobbled to a peg. The thunder roared as Jake stood and fired his old Paterson revolver at the braves, keeling one over as he hurled his lance. The Indians howled their fury and ran towards him. Jake fired indiscriminately, backing away. He reached the horse, jerked the peg from the ground, scrambled on to its back and, hanging low over her neck, viciously spurred her into a run. He went haring away across the prairie, vanishing into the darkness as huge blobs of rain began to fall.

Twelve

They didn't need to cast around for a trail. A cloud of buzzards hovering in the distance told them where they would find the scene of more carnage. As they drew near they could hear the odd coughing sounds of the red-hooded turkey vultures as they squabbled to breakfast on the bloody remains of three Comanche, and two white men. The big French poodle they had met at the foot of the pass who had chased after his mistress was barking forlornly. He was not used to being shot at. He loped along eagerly beside the Texan and the Wichita girl. Pete fired off a shot and the crowd of birds was sent chattering and hopping away.

The Swede and Jeb were both bloodily hairless and mutilated. With his boot Pete rolled over the old satchel of bones in his mangy fur. His face was drawn back in a rictus of pain, his lone tooth stabbing the air. The Texan stooped to go through his pockets. 'Nuthin',' he drawled. 'Somebody took it all. It ain't like Comanche to bother with bank notes.'

'Maybe the other man came back after they gone.'

'Maybe. That slippery rat sure ain't around here.' He didn't bother examining the Swede. It would be the same story. And he wasn't a pretty sight, that was for sure.

'C'mon,' he said. 'Let's ride.'

At least the women were still alive. The Comanche were probably planning to keep them as squaws, or sell them as slaves, either to other tribes, or down over the border to the *comancheros* for the bordellos of Mexico. Not a pleasant life.

Spotted Frog stared down at a fallen, painted Comanche sprawled in the grass. She made a down-turned grimace of fear.

'Red Bone's band.'

'Yeah, that ain't good news. You don't have to come.'

'I come,' she said, jumping back on her pony.

'One thang's fer sure,' he grinned. 'Life's gonna be mighty different for that princess. They don't have no champagne and caviar in a Comanch' encampment.'

Mad Jake had ridden hard through the storm until the hailstones forced him to jump down and pull his coat over his head, try to shelter. It had been an uncomfortable night. His instinct had been to put distance between himself and the Comanche but in the morning he had second thoughts. 'Them darn redskins musta got all them jewels, all that cash, all those decorations of the count. It's worth a fortune. I ain't goin' without that. Nobody's gonna say Mad Jake McGinty was sceered of a few lousy Injins.' It would be easy enough to follow their trail through the long damp grass. He would strike when they weren't expecting him. 'Sure am glad I brought some powder along,' he muttered, feeling in the capacious pockets of his overcoat for the powder horns.

Princess Sophie's dress was clinging to her. She had spent a dreadful night soaked to the skin by the downpour. At least it had deterred the Comanche from turning their attentions to her. They had huddled under their buffalo robes uncaring about the women. But how long that fate worse than death was to be withheld she had no idea. She was sore in heart, mind and body, sprawled over a pony, her wrists and ankles tied by rawhide encircling its belly, bouncing along helplessly like a piece of baggage. Marie was similarly roped to a cantering pony, jogging unceremoniously up and down. Sophie suddenly laughed, hysterically, in spite of her predicament. 'To think I joked to Captain Hazeltin that we might pretend to be captured by

Indians. That was really tempting fate.'

'God is always with us. Do not give up hope, milady,' her maid cried back.

'Yes?' Sophie tried to go with the rhythm of the hairy, smelly, uncomfortable pony, but it was difficult roped like that, the rawhide cutting into her skin, the horse's hide chafing her body. 'If so, He must certainly have an odd sense of humour.'

They travelled for miles across the grassland, her body burned by the sun and the wind, on and on all day, never ceasing. Her lips were parched with thirst. Hunger and fear gnawed at her insides. What were these savages going to do with them?

As the sun slid away through the golden-streaked clouds, like some glorious image of heaven in an ikon, the five warriors jumped from their horses. Red Bone had been riding Jeb's mustang, but was obviously not used to so bad-tempered a creature, nor the saddle and stirrups. He cut Sophie free and she tumbled down, her limbs so stiff she could hardly stand. He shouted something at her and gave her a push. She stood perplexed.

One of the Comanches had carried with him a piece of rope with a smouldering end. He used this to light some kindling of grass and twigs. 'I think they want us to find firewood,' Marie said, taking off her cape and draping it around her mistress's shoulders.

'Thank you, Marie.' Sophie tried to control her trembling limbs. 'Where can we find firewood? There are no trees in sight.'

Indeed, it was as if they were shipwrecked in a vast green ocean of wind-rustled grass, no port in sight. One of the Indians gave her another hard push and waved a clod of dung under her nose, pointing for her to go.

'They use it for the fire,' Marie cried. 'Dried buffalo dung. There must be some over there.'

Sure enough, they found some and

began to pile it in their arms. Sophie squealed with fright when she turned one heap over. There was a huge scorpion beneath, its vicious tail-barb coiled. She jumped back, dropping all she had, and began to sob. 'I can't bear it,' she howled.

'We must, my child.' Marie picked up the fallen chips. 'We must bear our suffering. If we anger them they will kill us.'

'Yes, yes, you are right.' Sophie blinked away her tears, carefully collected some more chips and returned to the five squatting warriors. They ignored the women. They had caught a tortoise and were intent on baking it in the ashes of the fire. Sophie collapsed in the grass and watched. It took a long time to cook. When it was done the Indians knifed at it, noisily. They contemptuously tossed the shell at the women. Sophie scraped with her nails to scoop up fleshy remains and passed the rest to Marie. It was not what she was used to, but it was surprisingly tasty. One of the Comanches tossed her a leather water bag and she gratefully licked up the trickle of brackish liquid. She even wiped a few drops across her forehead to try to revive herself.

The Comanches were talking together and passing a pipe of evil-smelling tobacco. The leader, with his bare, dark-sculpted shoulders, had his bow and quiver of arrows on his back, his lance and shield stuck in the ground. He had a long red bone through his hair quiff and was wearing only a dangling breechclout and knee-length moccasins. His body was covered with clay and red paint. There was a knife in a beaded sheath on his belt and dangling scalps. He glanced across at her and laughed, gutturally.

Red Bone had begun to inspect the contents of the gunny sack the three hunters had been carrying. He clipped Sophie's ruby necklace around his neck, tried on the matching bracelet. One of the Indians examined the count's cufflinks and medallions with delighted puzzlement. Another tried on Marie's veiled hat. The leader pulled out wads of dollars, shrugged, unimpressed and tossed them on the fire. Some bills began to burn, others fluttered away across the prairie. The other Comanches were busy attending to hobbling the horses. One gave a yelp of glee and pulled a bottle of whiskey from the late Swede's saddlebag. He jerked the cork with his teeth and took a swallow. The others jumped to their feet and demanded a swig.

Soon, as the rays of the sun flickered away they were shouting, laughing, staggering about, fighting for the last drops. They certainly couldn't hold their liquor. 'Oh, dear God! Look at them,' Sophie whispered. 'What are they going to do next?'

What they were planning to do became painfully apparent when Red Bone pointed at her, gave a scream, and grabbed hold of her. But the other Comanches wanted her, too. Two of them fought to pull her away, their scowling painted faces up close, as her shawl was torn off and her dress ripped apart in this drunken tug-of-war. Over their shoulder she glimpsed Marie getting similar treatment from the other two. Sophie fought back, but the air was pounded from her body as she was thrown to the ground. 'Oh, sweet Jesus,' she prayed. 'Help me.'

Mad Jake gave a low whistle as he watched the cavorting antics of the whiskey-crazed Comanches against the fire's glow. 'The dirty savages,' he growled, in righteous indignation that they were intent on what he, too, wanted. 'You keep your filthy hands off that princess. She's mine.'

He had kept a good mile behind as he trailed the Comanches. His horse did not kick up dust on the rain damp ground so he avoided detection. Now it was easy to creep up on them once they had started on the whiskey and the women, scrapping among themselves, caterwauling and falling about the flames. 'I'll fix you, you heathen,' he muttered. 'No way you havin' the cash and jewels *and* the gals.'

He pulled out one of his powder horns. He emptied into his coat pocket the two leather pouches of coins he had taken from the corpses of the Swede and Jeb when he had returned to them. He filled the pouches with gunpowder and attached short fuses to them. The Comanches had momentarily thrown the females aside. It looked like one of them had found another bottle, probably in Jeb's pack. They were fighting and swaying about the fire trying to glug it back. 'Have fun,' Jake grunted. *'Adios, amigos.'*

He hurled the first pouch at the fire. It didn't need the lit fuse for it landed right in the flames. Ker-ash! The explosion blew one of the Comanches into the air, parting his extremities from his trunk.

A lump of flesh hit Jake in the face. 'Eugh!' he said, and wiped it away. The other four had been blown off their feet by the blast, or seen the smouldering pouch and leapt clear in time. They were getting to their feet, looking stunned and groggy. Should he give them his second bomb? No, no time. He pulled his revolver, but he couldn't keep a steady aim.

'Hang on to the hosses,' Black Pete shouted at Spotted Frog, leaping down and tossing her the mare's reins. They had heard the women's screams, seen the Comanches in silhouette against the flames cavorting about as they approached. And then the eruption of the fire. 'We don't want no more funerals on this picnic, leastways not on our side.'

He drew both his Smith and Wesson self cockers, and strode towards the fire. What in hell had gone up, maybe a powder horn? One of the Indians had a carbine in his hands. He had to get to them. They would be mad enough now to kill the girls. He was still sixty paces away. He had to try a long shot. He raised his right-hand

.32 and took out the one with the carbine, hitting him in the shoulder, spinning him back into the flames.

Jake was about to squeeze the trigger of his Paterson when he saw the flash of gunfire from the darkness on the far side of the fire, saw one of the Comanches topple back. 'Who in hell?' he muttered.

The Texan, like some ghost out of the war in his grey frockcoat, strode steadily forward. His second revolver spat fire and another Comanche collapsed, clutching at his chest. A third Comanche hurled a lance. The tall man stepped aside, unflinching, and his left-hand weapon spurted death.

'Hell and Lucifer!' Jake was awestruck. 'I ain't never seen shooting like that.'

Red Bone had a carbine in his hands but he seemed unsure how to use it, pumping the lever, aiming from the hip with no result. He didn't know he had to operate the hammer, too. With a scream of rage he hurled the weapon at the Texan, leapt across the fire and on to a pony, swirling it away into the darkness. In the sudden silence after the shooting they could hear the hooves' drumbeats heading away.

'Them useless coyotes tol' me he was killed,' Jake growled. 'Well, he soon will be.'

Ka-dang! The slug bounced off a rock and put another hole through Pete's frockcoat, grazing his thigh. Immediately he returned fire with the double-actions aiming at the flash of gunfire.

'Jeesis shee-t!' Jake ducked as lead whined about him perilously close for comfort. He began to crawl away through the grass to where he had hobbled the paint. 'I'm gittin' outa here.' He scrambled into the saddle, spurred the quarter-horse viciously, and lit out after Red Bone. 'I'll catch up with Bowen some other time.'

Black Pete stood listening. 'Both the varmints gone,' he muttered.

Sophie, nearly naked, her dress tattered, was crawling towards him. She pointed a shaking finger. 'Look out!' she screamed.

Pete turned and saw the shoulder-shot Comanche, his eyes burning angrily through the war paint, raising his carbine to shoot. He put him down with a heart shot from his left-hand and a second from his right-hand to make sure. The scent of burning powder in his nostrils, he went over and poked him with his boot, with as much compassion as he would have for a mad dog. 'He's dead,' he drawled in his sawtooth Texan accent. 'They all dead. An' I don't fancy them other two'll be back. You're safe now.'

Sophie stared at him, fair hair tangled over her face, her eyes filled with fear. 'Who *are* you?'

'C'mon.' He bolstered his guns, and put a gloved hand out to her as if he was coaxing a cat in from the cold. 'I ain't gonna hurt you. Ah'm a former marshal and bounty hunter. Your brother sent me to look for you. You are Princess Sophie, aincha?'

'Yes.' Sophie stood upright, trying to

shield her pale-skinned body with the torn dress as she saw the man's dark eyes smouldering over her. 'I am she. My maid is over there. You had better go reassure her.'

'Looks like you've had a rough deal.' He spoke gruffly, intending it kindly, but he couldn't help a flicker of lust as he saw a tremble of pink-tipped breast protruding from the girl's bodice. He'd been in the desert a long time. She sure was some looker even in her torn and troubled state. He stared at her, put out a hand, stroked the hair from her cheek. And turned on his heel. 'What'n hell am I thinkin' of?' he said as he went to look for the maid.

Spotted Frog arrived with the horses as he carried Marie in. She was in a bad state, mostly shock and panic. He laid her down gently by the fire. 'She'll be OK once she's had some sleep,' he said. 'I sure am plumb tuckered out myself, same as the horses must be. I figure we'll be all right here. It's too damn dark to move on.'

'Won't they come back?' Sophie asked, sharply.

'Naw. They've had a bellyful.' He went to the grey, pulled a blanket from behind the saddle, threw it to her. 'Here, cover that pretty hide of yourn 'fore I forgit I'm an officer an' a gentleman.'

Spotted Frog gave him a curious look, followed by a baleful one at the white woman. Yes, her skin was white, whiter than any skin she had seen before. She rekindled the fire, found their coffee pot, crushed beans with a carbine butt, tipped in water from Pete's wooden canteen. 'He wants her more than he wants me,' she murmured sadly, as she squatted in her blanket and buckskins. 'I can see it in his eyes.'

'What are you going to do with us?' Sophie asked.

'Send you back to your brother, I guess.'

'Huh, a fat lot he cares.'

'Jest because he set off to save his own skin don't mean he didn't care about'cha.

He did the wisest thang.' Pete rolled a quirley, lit up with a burning twist of grass, and breathed out acrid smoke with a grimace of satisfaction. He kicked at a broken bottle. 'Sure is a shame they finished off all that whiskey.'

'They burned the money,' Sophie said.

'Hot damn.' Pete poked at the charred remains.

'Look!' The Indian gal thrust a green dollar bill under his nose. 'Wind blow across prairie.'

Pete studied them. 'Fresh-minted. Our glorious new president's head. Ulysses Grant. To think I fought against him and his horde at Shiloh. Maybe we can collect a few more in the marnin'? Guess it all belongs to the count.'

'If you find any keep them,' Sophie said. 'For rescuing us.'

'Gee, thanks.' Pete tucked it in his pocket with a wide grin. 'Thass more than gen'rous.'

'You'll find some of my trinkets on

those dead Indians.' Sophie shuddered as she stared at the Comanche sprawled in the stiff frieze of death. 'The rest should be in that sack.'

Pete took a look and retrieved various rings, bracelets, and necklaces of precious stones. And Marie's hat. He threw it to her. 'This yours?' She nodded, dumbly, and held it in her hands. He pulled the Comanche out by their ankles and laid them in the dark. 'The coyotes can have 'em,' he said.

He made a couch of two of their buffalo robes. 'There y'are, your ladyship. A nice soft bed. If I were you I'd snuggle up with your maid and Frog here. It's turning cold.'

The days were still mild, but he sniffed at the wind, yes, there was a hint of snow. Winter was coming on. He poured two tin mugs of coffee and passed them to the Russians. Then looked through the contents of the gunny sack. He gave a whistle at the sight of more baubles, bangles and beads, pouches of gold dust and some silver coin. 'Whoo! It's lucky for you them Injins ain't got much idea of the value of these thangs. Waal, Princess, it looks like it's mostly all here.' He tossed the sack to her.

'No.' She shook her head, staring fixedly across the steaming mug as she sipped at it. 'My most precious pieces are on that one who got away.'

'Red Bone?'

'Yes, the leader of them, whatever he's called. He has my ruby necklace, ring and bracelet. Those stones are priceless. They are the Countess Ekterina's rubies. They were on loan to me. I must get them back.'

'You must, mustcha?' Pete glowered at the dainty Russian girl, with her tangle of blonde hair, her little upturned nose and pointed chin. Her ruby lips pouted, she had the look of one born to be obeyed. 'I guess that means me.'

'I will pay you two thousand dollars

reward if you retrieve them for me. You need cash, don't you?'

'Yeah, I guess that's true. Finished?' He held out a hand for the tin mug. 'Me and Frog could do with a cup ourselves. We've all had a hard ride.'

'So,' the princess asked, 'what are you going to do?'

'What I figure is Frog can see you two back to Fort Sill. Me, I'll go on after Red Bone. An' that other varmint who took a pot at me. Reckon it was Jake McGinty. Me an' him's got a score to settle an' he's still, I hope, got my cash and my pack horse.'

'No,' Frog said, her dark eyes on him. 'I don't like white women. I want come with you, Pete.'

'Do me a favour, Frog. Jest guide 'em back to the fort. Then go stay with your people. I'll meet you there in, say, half a moon. OK?'

'OK.' She shrugged and stared into her coffee. 'If you say.'

'So, now you three better git some shut-eye. I'll keep watch for a bit.'

'If you don't mind,' Sophie said, in a lowered voice, 'I'd rather not have her sleeping next to me.'

'Why not?' Pete flared up. 'Because she's an Injin? She's as good as you, your ladyship. Iffen not better.'

'I—I just feel creepy just to see one of them. I can't tell you what we've been through.'

'Come on Frog, we'd better sleep t'other side of the fire. We ain't wanted over here.'

They lay together for a long while, leaning against his saddle, on top of his tarpaulined soogans which shielded against the prairie damp, staring at the flickering flames, or up at the murky sky, a half-moon occasionally glimpsed through the tumbling clouds.

'Yeah,' he said. 'It sure is gonna snow. What'll you do when winter comes, Frog?'

'I do not know.' She nestled into him,

her blanket around her shoulders. 'Perhaps I will stay with my family.'

'Mebbe there ain't no point in me moseying back to Texas? Mebbe that li'l Spanish gal I bin thinkin' about is jest a dream.' He put an arm loosely around her shoulders. 'Good-looker like her's probably hitched by now. This sure is fine country. What do I wanta leave fer? A man could make a living as a guide or a hunter. He could even raise a family and a few cows. Build a cabin in the woods. Live peaceful-like.'

Spotted Frog's face widened into a smile and she beamed up at him, hesitantly. She slipped her fingers inside his shirt, to flutter against his hard-muscled abdomen. 'How is your wound?' she whispered.

'It's healing nicely. I reckon a little extra nocturnal activity wouldn't do it no harm.' He looked across at the two figures bundled in the buffalo robes. They appeared to be sleeping like babes. He glanced down at Frog and grinned. 'You ever heard of the white man's quaint old custom of kissing?'

'What is that?'

'No, I guess the varmints you went with were in too much of a hurry to bother.' He turned over to her and dipped his head close to her face, began unpicking the buttons of her blouse. 'You kinda put your lips together, see, like this.' His hard, horny hand cupped around the softness of her tattooed breast. 'Mmm,' he murmured. 'That's nice. Now, what next? I fergit.'

'You make my bells tinkle,' she smiled, wriggling up under him and clasping his waist with her legginged-legs. 'You make them tinkle long as you like.'

Thirteen

The pipes and drums of the band of the Seventh Cavalry led the column of troopers and horse-drawn howitzers into Fort Sill and at their head was Lt. Gen. Philip Sheridan, who had been put in command of the Missouri Division, which included the whole of Indian Territory. By his side was his young protégé, Lt. Col. George Custer, acting commander of the regiment, with his shoulder-length russet-gold hair, and dandified costume, the very picture of a dashing cavalier on his white charger. For the trappers, tame Indians, and civilians who watched their arrival it was a stirring sight, the colours flying, the band fluting 'Garry Owen'.

'It's the general,' Captain Hazeltin muttered with some dismay, as he sat his horse in front of his men and saluted them. 'Where's he sprung from?'

The famed war leader and disciplinarian, Sheridan gave a dour glance at the black soldiers of the Tenth. A stout, ruddy-complexioned man, he climbed stiffly from his horse, stroked his bushy moustache and led the way into Hazeltin's office.

'I wasn't informed of your arrival, sir,' Hazeltin said, ushering the general into his own chair, feeling distinctly nervous.

'No, I don't suppose you were,' Sheridan replied, gruffly. 'I'm making a tour of the frontier forts. Decided to inspect the newest outpost first so rode along with my friend Custer here.'

Custer unbuckled his long sabre and clattered it to one side, offering his white-gauntleted hand to Hazeltin. 'No need to get in a fluster, Captain. We've arrived early, I know. You're still in the chair for another week. In the meantime I'll acclimatize myself.'

'What you got in the way of a belly-

193

warmer?' the general demanded. 'We've had a damn cold ride.'

'Kentucky bourbon, sir?' Hazeltin hurried to produce a bottle from a cupboard and poured two glasses. He tried not to show the shaking of his hand. 'For you, Colonel?'

'Never touch the stuff,' Custer said, taking a chair and thrusting out his long, high-booted legs. He cast aside his campaign hat and stroked his long hair into place with a conceited smile. 'Nor the evil weed.'

'Don't know how to relax, that's your trouble, George,' Sheridan grunted. 'When's the wife arriving?'

'Wednesday, by hack from Fort Gibson. Libby's looking forward to my new command.'

'Your quarters will be ready for you by then, Colonel. You caught me a little off guard.'

'No hurry, old boy. Don't want to push you out.'

'It is an honour to meet you, sir.'

'Well, Hazeltin, what's it like being in charge of a collection of blacks?'

'They're a fine body of men, sir, good horsemen, eager and alert. I'll introduce you at dinner to my officers.'

'You mean we've got to have 'em dine with us?'

'Now then, George, no need for those sentiments. This is the new army now.'

'We're going to be awful crowded in the fort before we pull out,' Hazeltin said. 'I hope we don't have any incidents.'

'You mean fights?' Custer smiled. 'Surely you can control your men?'

'Of course, sir, but they don't take insults lying down.'

'Come, come, we've more important matters to discuss,' Sheridan said. 'I need to take a close look at your log, Captain. Your accounts ...'

The wide parade ground was a scene of much bustle as the new arrivals fed and watered their horses, erected Sibley tents as temporary accommodation prior to the Tenth vacating their cabins, and sorted out their ammunition and supplies.

Suddenly the lookout shouted a warning and the stockade gates were opened. The soldiers saw a little man in a mud-splattered white uniform, fair hair and a goatee beard come galloping wildly through. 'My servants all killed, my sister kidnapped,' he gabbled out.

'Count!' Captain Hazeltin ran out to him. 'What's happened? Where's Sophie?'

'Zose guides you gave me. Zey turned on us. It was murder. Zey stole all my money, my jewels. Zey took her. I was lucky to escape with my life.'

'Took her! Oh, my God! I should never have left you alone.'

General Sheridan had come out on to the veranda. 'What's going on? What's all the racket about?'

'Sir, this is Count Alexis, of Russia. He was leading a hunting party. His sister, the Princess Sophie, has been snatched. She—she is my betrothed. I beg permission to lead my men in search of her.'

'Hang on a minute. You'd better bring him inside. Let's try to make sense of this garbled nonsense, Captain. You'd better give him a bourbon. Looks like he needs one. Has he been shot?' He pointed to the crimson stain across the count's waistcoat.

'No, no! Zat is vere my butler spilled ze cranberry sauce.'

Captain Hazeltin and his platoon of black troopers rode hard out of Fort Sill up through Blue Beaver Creek, along past Ketch Lake and Frenchman's Lake. Regulations required that they rested every thirty miles for their horses' sakes and the captain was in a fever of agitation until, before dawn, they were on their way again.

It was as they neared the Sunset Pool they saw them, Sophie, her maid, and the Wichita girl. Uncaring about the watching troopers Captain Hazeltin caught Sophie in his arms as she tumbled from her mount, squeezed her to him and smothered her in kisses. 'You poor child,' he said. 'What have they done to you?'

'Oh, Franklin,' she murmured, 'it was terrible.'

In the morning they retrieved the count's wagons and turned back towards the fort. Sophie was eager to assure the captain that 'the worst had not occurred' while in the Comanches' hands. 'We had a narrow escape,' she said.

Once back at Fort Sill, introduced to General Sheridan and Custer, Sophie made a rapid recovery and was soon flouncing around in her silk dresses as if she hadn't a care in the world, showing her engagement ring to Mrs Custer and the other officers' wives.

'We are going to be married in Tucson,' she told them. 'Franklin is riding down with his men and I will go by the Butterfield Overland Stage.'

'You poor girl,' Mrs Custer cried. 'One

of the most desolate trails there is. What an awful posting.'

'I don't mind,' Sophie said. 'You always accompany your husband, so I will mine.'

Everybody thought what a brave creature she was, as spunky as hell. When the Tenth moved out of the fort they had spent so much time building to set out on the long journey to Arizona, there was much shouting of commands, bugle blowing and flag-waving. Captain Hazeltin led the march past General Sheridan, Sophie fluttered her lace handkerchief and dabbed it to her eyes. The captain could hardly prevent the tears brimming to his own as he left behind the girl he loved.

She will be all right, he said to himself He had given her a cheque for $2,000 as Sophie had explained that with all the count's paper money burned by the Comanche they had only a small amount of gold dust and silver to see them through. That would amply cover her expenses and trousseau until they met in Tucson.

Fourteen

'You say some frontiersmen secured your escape from the Comanche, Princess?' George Custer prompted as they sat at dinner in the officers' mess.

'Yes, a tall man with a black beard, very wild-looking,' Sophie said, glad to be the heroine of the tale. 'A Texan in a bullet-holed grey coat. The Indian girl who guided us back said his name was Black Pete. I promised him a reward if he retrieves my rubies for me, so he has gone after Red Bone.'

'It's us who should be after him, General,' Custer told Sheridan, who presided at the head of table. 'I'm preparing a punitive expedition against these Comanche. We'll hang them, every one, I promise you, Princess.'

'Oh, there's only that Red Bone man left. The others are dead.'

'There's plenty more of the red devils skulking in their lairs out on the prairie,' Custer said. 'Red Bone's one of the Kwahadi band, ain't he? Same as Quannah Parker's gang.'

'It's time these savages were taught they can't go round treating civilized people, not to say renowned foreign guests, like this,' Sheridan grunted. 'Hit 'em hard, George.'

Custer preened his long moustaches and flicked dust from his unique black-velvet cavalry coat, trimmed with gold braid, his wide collared shirt with a silver star on either side. Unlike the other formally dressed officers arranged in pecking order down the long table he wore a scarlet bandanna slung loosely around his throat. 'I can assure you, General, there'll be no kid-glove treatment while I'm in charge of this fort.'

Apart from their difference in age and

dress, he and Sheridan were two of a kind. Both had passed out bottom of their class from military academy, but rose to high rank during the Civil War due to their spectacular bravery and initiative in battle. Both showed little mercy to their defeated enemy. Both were agreed the day of the red man was over. Both were brashly insubordinate to their superiors. Both considered themselves above ordinary mortals. Their lust for power and self-publicity verged on insane megalomania.

Custer's wife Elizabeth was a somewhat severe and Germanic-looking blonde, sitting on Sheridan's left beside the count. This time there was no caviar and champagne but plain frontier food. Sophie, on the general's right, beside Custer, had retrieved most of her expensive wardrobe and, in a dress of white silk, her ringleted fair hair clasped by a diadem, she sparkled as the centre of attention and drew more admiring glances than any of the other officers' wives.

As the company ate, Sheridan and Custer monopolized the conversation, very fond of their own voices. They reminisced on about the Shenandoah Valley campaign, Fisher's Hill, Five Forks, and how the wild Reb cavalry leader Jeb Stuart had been killed in one of Custer's charges.

'Is it true you were made a general at twenty-three?' Sophie asked, her dress rustling as she turned to him.

George Custer gave a deprecating flourish of his hand. 'The youngest since the Frenchie, Lafayette.'

His icy-blue eyes met her sky-blue ones unflinchingly. They, too, were rather alike in their blondness and arrogance. Sophie gave him a secret smile, for she had been swotting up on his career. 'Franklin tells me your brigade's heroic charge at Gettysburg greatly contributed to that victory.'

'True,' Sheridan butted in. 'His bravery earned him promotion.'

'Yes, sir,' Custer replied. 'But it was your stubborn command that cut off Lee's retreat at Appomattox.'

'We showed 'em a thing or two, eh, Colonel?'

Custer flinched slightly for he hated the title. It still rankled that he had been reduced to Lieutenant Colonel in the reshuffle after the war. The severe drop in salary had not been pleasant, either. Most men sucked up to him by still calling him General. 'We certainly did,' he grunted.

'Vell, I am feeling a little peaky. If you vill exscuse please I vill retire early. Are you coming, Sophie?'

'Oh, must I? Cannot I stay a little longer? I do so love to hear General Custer's tales of adventure. So exciting!'

'Well, I've heard them before,' Elizabeth Custer sighed. 'So, I, too, will retire.'

Sheridan glowered at Sophie. 'It is the custom for ladies to withdraw at this point so we gentlemen can enjoy bourbon and cigars.'

'Oh!' Sophie pouted her pretty lips. 'Do we have to have all those stuffy rules? I thought on the frontier we would be more free. Can't I stay a short while? I'd love to hear how you cleared the Rebs from the Shenandoah Valley, General.'

'Well, if you put it like that.' Sheridan beamed and patted her hand. 'Why not?'

The company rose as Custer escorted his wife out, followed by the count. 'I'll be back to listen to that,' the colonel smiled.

He returned in a short while and he and Sheridan regaled her and the officers with more of their exploits as the whiskey was passed round. Sophie, herself, laughingly imbibed a glass or two, the life and soul of the party. 'It is so good to be back safe,' she said, 'and among such fine gentlemen.' She gave a little yawn. 'I think I should be off to bed now.'

'I will see you to your quarters, Princess.' Custer rose and bowed gallantly. 'I'll return for a hand of cards, General.'

He took her arm as they walked across the dark parade ground. 'So, you're to marry Captain Hazeltin? Just as well I should think.'

'What do you mean, sir?'

'Well, you know, camp gossip. It gets to a commander's ears.'

'Really?' Sophie looked up at him and tried to tug her arm away, but he held her tight. 'And what does camp gossip say?'

'You and he having a high old time in the woods.'

'You, sir, are no gentleman!' Sophie spun on him, trying to pound him with her fists, but he hung on tight, and thrust her into the darkness of an alleyway between two cabins, pressing her up tight against a log wall. 'Leave me alone!' she cried.

'Is that what you want, Princess?'

'Please!' She was breathing hard. 'Don't be like this. It is true Franklin and I were a little indiscreet. He is a sweet boy. But that doesn't mean—'

'Of course. Don't get me wrong, Princess. I adore my wife, Libby.' He relaxed his grip and stroked her hair from her brow. 'But a man such as I cannot be confined to one woman alone. I enjoy female company. Their favours, you might say.'

'Really? That's big of you, General.' She looked up at him in the light cast from a lamp through a window, cosying herself into him in the shadows. She gave him a little toothy smile, fluttered her eyelashes, as if to brush away tears, and asked, 'If you want a favour of me, would *you* do *me* a favour in return, General?'

'Such as?'

'It's just that, well, we are practically destitute out here. We have been robbed of our cash and my most precious jewels. My brother is in dire need of some ready money but he is too proud to ask for a loan. But, I—'

'How much?'

'Oh, three thousand dollars. A mere bagatelle.'

'Three thousand? You don't come cheap.'

Sophie sniffled and gave another cheeky smile. 'Should I? I *am* betrothed, General. It's only to see us through to the bank at Santa Fe. My brother has to travel in style.'

'Hmm?' He contemplated her like a cat the cream. 'What collateral can you give me?'

Sophie pulled the diadem from her golden hair, which tumbled like a shiny waterfall to her shoulders. 'This, I can assure you, is worth twice that amount. You will return it when we repay the loan. And that will be done as soon as we reach civilization and reestablish ourselves.'

Custer ran his hands down her breasts, down to her slim waist and her hips, and gave a reckless grin. He was an inveterate gambler and liked to take a chance. And he had never played for a princess before. 'Come to my office in the morning,' he murmured, as he kissed her. 'I will lend you the cash.'

'That's a promise?'

'Princess, Custer would never go back on his word.'

And then it was suddenly as if into the excitement of a cavalry charge. 'Tally Ho! Off and Away!' Princess Sophie threaded her fingers into his long blond hair and sighed, 'Oh, General, you mustn't...you mustn't.'

'I must,' he gasped.

Fifteen

Great seething black clouds of silver-edged cumuli seemed to be rising from the prairie so Pete guessed he must be approaching a high ridge. He slid from his grey and crept forward, peering over a cliff edge down into a deep valley. 'Great Jehosophat!' He gave a whistle of surprise for there must have been some hundred tipis clustered along the sides of a stream that trickled through the canyon. 'So this is their hidey-hole?'

It was early dawn and only a few youths were about attending to the ponies, and old women collecting firewood to cook the morning meals. Smoke from the tipis drifted across the terrain. In some ways it was an idyllic scene, the unchanged way these people had lived for centuries. And in other ways it struck an icy chill through him. 'How in tarnation am I gonna extricate Red Bone from this crowd?'

The Texan hesitated some while. His heart had begun thudding in his ribcage. No man ever rode into a Comanche camp without a tingling in his scalp and a shivery feeling down his spine. He was tempted to turn tail, go back. But he was never one to give up on something that he had started. And he sure would be loath to go home empty-handed. 'Aw, hell,' he groaned. 'We ain't at war, are we? Come on, less go.' He searched for a path down the steep ridge-side and led the grey down.

Suddenly a shrill scream told him he had been spotted, probably by one of the sleepy guards posted around the camp. By then he had reached rideable ground, so he swung back on the grey and spurred her towards a group of warriors who had leapt on their ponies and were charging towards him with blood-curdling cries. He gritted his teeth and rode steadily on towards them.

'Hai-yaiee!' a feathered Comanche yelped, swirling his pony to a halt before him, brandishing a coup stick from which dangled scalps, as the rest surrounded him. 'What do you want here?' he shouted in Comanche.

'I come to see Red Bone.' Pete spoke slowly in their language, keeping his guns holstered, ignoring their aggressive threats, jeers and jostling. 'He has stolen something of ourn. We want it back.'

The warriors stalked around him, curiously, poking him with their lance tips, or brandishing their weapons in his face. Pete remained impassive. 'I ain't got no quarrel with none of you. Just Red Bone.'

The savage, scowling faces suddenly creased into laughter at this white man's audacity. 'We could kill you out-of-hand, like a fly. Nobody would care,' the one with the coup stick shouted.

'True, you could. But I have come with

a challenge to Red Bone. It is he who should decide on that.'

The Comanche chattered among themselves, then screamed with excitement and escorted Pete on towards the camp. The dogs barked and the children ran along beside them pointing at the strange white man. Squaws came from their tipis to stare up at him as he passed. They surrounded him as he came to a halt. 'I will tell Red Bone,' the coup stick warrior called.

'Mighty fine.' Pete tried to relax, grinning down at the kids, tossing a plug of baccy at one of the braves. 'You tell him Black Pete is here.'

They were a dark-skinned, wild-looking race, most of the men bare-legged in spite of the cold, in tattered skins, or buffalo-capes, with their bows and quivers, or ancient muskets held in readiness. An old man, wearing a kind of pillbox hat made of straw, peered up at him. 'Black Pit, I remember you,' he quavered out. 'You fought with the grey-coats against the blue-coats. You led the Cherokee.'

'That's right,' he gritted out. It would do no harm to remind them he was no lover of the federal army. He offered his hand to the old man, who took it in both his and shook it, warmly. 'I have killed plenty blue-coats in my time.'

The Comanche with the coup stick returned. 'Red Bone will see you,' he shouted.

Some Indians just didn't know how to speak quietly, Pete reflected, as he pushed his horse through the noisy crowd towards a tipi that stood in isolation.

He stepped down and into its dim interior. As many of the warriors as could crowded in after him. 'So far, so good,' he muttered, and through the gloom made out a Comanche seated cross-legged on the far side of the fire. His thighs were lithe and muscled, and he wore a breastplate of porcupine quills, a buckskin jacket hung with scalps, much wampum around his neck, and a couple of eagle feathers dangling from his hair. If hair you could call it. It was caked with dried mud into which a dyed red bone had been inserted. The warrior's face was painted with downward red and white stripes and the look in his eyes was ... well ... hostile might be the word.

'Texan,' he intoned in Comanche, 'why do you dare to come here? You have killed many of my men. Their wives, sisters and mothers grieve here. You deserve the slow death.'

There was a sigh at this remark as the Indians thought of the torture that might be inflicted. Pete rolled himself a cigarette and offered it to Red Bone, who shook his head. He did not want any offer of peace or friendship.

Pete lit up, puffed out smoke and said, 'I killed them because you attacked me and later because you had stolen our women. There is something else you have stolen that we want back.' He pointed to the ruby necklace amid the other 'magic' around

Red Bone's neck, the bracelet and ruby ring on his finger. 'Give me them back and I will go in peace.'

Red Bone gave a scoffing laugh. 'You will go nowhere. How will you go when I have cut off your legs?'

'Sure, and then my arms, and then my head. That would appeal to a coward like you.'

There was another gasp of dismay at his words. How did he dare to speak like this? Red Bone leaped to his feet, his knife drawn, as if about to jump across the fire at him. He was snarling and spitting out words like an angry cougar.

The old Indian in the pill-box hat had squeezed into the inner circle and held up his arms for quiet. 'This man is Black Pit, the grey-coat warrior. He has been an enemy of the blue-coats. We should give him a hearing.'

'The grey-coats are no longer at war with the blue-coats,' another put in. 'Now they turn on us. All white men are the same.'

'He is not the same. No other white man would dare to ride alone into a Comanche camp and make these demands,' the old man said. 'I say we should not kill him. I say it is up to Red Bone to kill him.'

There was an excited shout at this for all warriors liked to watch a fight. This had become a question of honour. 'Fair enough,' Pete said. 'You reckon you're good with a knife, Red Bone? Good. I challenge you. Hand-to-hand combat.' He took out his own knife and stuck it in the turf. 'You win, you keep them blood-red trinkets. I win, I take 'em and go.'

He took the cigarette from his dry lips and tossed it into the fire. What kinda fool thing was he proposing? The odds against him beating Red Bone were pretty steep, especially with that recent wound in his chest. And would he accept?

'White men, I do not trust them. I say we kill him now,' Red Bone growled. 'This is some kind of trick.'

'So you are yellow. You only good

for raping defenceless girls and scalping dead, white men? That was a fool thing to do, Red Bone. Custer will be looking for vengeance.'

'Custer?' the old man asked with alarm. 'Yellow Hair?'

'Yeah. Hear tell he's been posted to Fort Sill. You give back that property that don't belong to you, maybe I can meet up with him, tell him this matter's all been sorted out.'

Red Bone had squatted back on his haunches, bristling with anger. The dark eyes watched him, expectantly. There were sneers on the faces of some of the warriors. He had been accused of cowardice. There was no way he could squirm out of this.

'We will fight,' he shouted.

There was a great clamour. The people pushed out of the tipi and gathered in a circle in the centre of the camp. Pete took off his caped greatcoat and tossed it over the grey. He unbuckled his guns and handed them to the old man. He would have had more ease of movement if he had taken off his shotgun chaps but he didn't have time. He wanted to get this over with, one way or the other. He stripped off his shirt and stood bare-chested, tall and broad-shouldered. Red Bone stood across from him, nearly naked, making some sort of chant to the skies. Pete glanced up at the heavens. Maybe it was the last time he would ever do so. It was a good day to die. He spat on his hands and gripped hold of the long-bladed Bowie of best Solingen steel, sharp as a scalpel.

'Hai!' Red Bone leapt towards him. Pete edged away. The two men circled each other like a couple of scorpions, their knives poised. 'Ha!' Red Bone's knife swung and stabbed, viciously. Pete parried him. Red Bone lunged. His knife slit the bandage from Pete's chest and the silent crowd gasped to see the blue and scarlet wound exposed, but he did not draw blood. Desperately Pete went on the attack, slashing like he had a sabre in his hand. Red Bone spun aside, kicked out at the wound and sent Pete tumbling, pain searing through him. He gripped his chest tight and rolled to his knees, saw the flash of a knife felt the slice across his throat, and rolled away again. Red Bone picked up dust and tossed it in his face. Semi-blinded, Pete ducked as Red Bone charged at him. He tossed the Comanche over his shoulder and spun round to face him again. The knife whistled back and forth as Pete backed to avoid it by a hair's breadth. Suddenly Red Bone flung the knife, aiming at the wound. By the luck of the gods Pete that second tripped. As he fell the knife nearly parted his hair. This wasn't playing fair. Red Bone had pulled a tomahawk from his belt and, with screams of anger, was flailing it at him. Pete caught his arm and kicked his boot up into his gut. The Comanche went down and Pete trod on his arm, gripped him by the throat, his knife raised. He looked around.

The Comanches stood as if in a trance.

'Kill him!' one shouted. 'He is yours.'

Pete looked at the eyes flickering through the paint like a snake's. He had him pinned by his knees on his arms, his hand squeezing his throat. He plunged the knife into Red Bone's jugular and the blood squirted like a fountain.

There was a great cry from the assembled Indians as he stood up, but a cry somehow forlorn and sad. He looked at them to see if they were going to give any trouble, and wiped his knife. He slid it back into its sheath, stooped and ripped the jewels from the dead warrior's neck, wrist and finger. He held them aloft as a sign of victory and returned to his horse.

'It was a near thing,' he grunted, wiping away blood trickling from the cut to his neck. 'He nearly got me.' He tied his bandanna tight around the cut, put on his shirt, hide waistcoat, and frockcoat and buckled his gunbelt.

The old man in the pill-box hat handed him his stiff-brimmed stetson. 'Black Pit,

I will ride with you from our village back towards your hills to give you safe conduct in case we meet any of our war parties.'

'Thanks,' he drawled, mounting up, and riding away through the staring crowd of Comanche. Bow-legged and bitter-looking they were the ugliest of the Plains Indians. But once on horseback they were a force to be reckoned with, even with their primitive stone-age weapons. He couldn't help but admire their determination to fight on against all the odds.

'Ain't you ever thought of coming in, settling down in the Territory like the other tribes?' he asked as they rode.

'They are cowards to seek peace with the white man,' the old man replied.

'Well, if you people had any sense, now Red Bone is gone, you would stop raiding and make peace, too. There ain't no way you can win.'

'This is our land,' the Comanche said, with a shrug. 'Sometimes there is nothing else to do but fight.'

Sixteen

'Hear the wind howl,' he muttered, and pulled his bullet-notched hat down over his narrowed eyes. He clenched his jaw against the bitterly cold wind and forced the grey's head into the gale. 'Hear the wind blow, gal. We're in line for a blizzard. Sure, I know you'd rather drift south towards Texas but we gotta go thisaway.'

Flecks of sleet hit his face stinging like sharp pins, the wind wailing around him like witches trying to tear him from his mount. No wonder the Indians believed in all those spirits living out in a place like this. The north wind. The wind that kills they call it. It comes roaring down across the plains from the cold Canadian provinces. He cut back across it, trying to judge if he was on the right course for the gap.

Gradually the sleet turned to snow as the light waned, plastering the front of his coat, his face and beard with ice, congealing his eyes so he could hardly see. 'C'mon, gal,' he shouted out, giving her a whack, urging her on. An instinct led him, more than a faint memory of the maps of the Territory he had pored over in the war.

When it was too dark to see any more he dug a hole in the snow-covered grass, pulled up the collar of his greatcoat, and huddled shivering in his rubber-blanket. He had no fuel to make a fire. He chewed on meat jerky and took a swallow of icy water. He gave the mare a handful of split-corn. It should keep her going. She could paw through the snow for grazing. All they could do was shiver through the long night and wait for it to pass.

With daylight Pete saw that he was covered by a layer of snow. He dug himself out. At least the sun was shining. The prairie was a glistening layer of ice through which tufts of grass poked. Pete flapped his arms and stamped his boots to bring back some warmth and circulation. The mare had drifted off half a mile away, hardly discernible against the snow.

He gave her a whistle and she started trotting back to him. 'There's the mountains,' he said to her. 'Thass where we gotta go.' He slung on the wood and hide California saddle, tightened the cinch, and climbed aboard. 'Giddup, gal. Ain't no use hangin' around. We ain't got no breakfast today.'

He brushed the snow from his coat and set off in a beeline towards the gap in the hills, on towards the blue mountains.

Mad Jake McGinty had been headed across the prairie intent on reaching New Mexico when he had seen the rider coming though the darkness the night before. He had made a hasty withdrawal, turning back in his tracks. He guessed he could have hunkered down and let the Texan pass,

225

but that wasn't his way. He had a score to settle. He still had the Texan's wads of greenback dollars, the $2,000 he had kept from Jeb and the Swede, tucked inside his shirt. He wasn't planning on parting with them. That bastard had it coming, and this time there would be no mistake.

He was a nuisance, that was for sure. But it had to be done. Jake had ridden back through the night, and by dawn had located Burford Gap. He swore, foully, as he rode up the canyon looking for a good place to hide. In fact, Jake McGinty cursed Black Pete up hill and down dale, cursed his mother and his sisters, if he had any, and his future progeny, cursed him for being alive, and cursed Jeb and the Swede for not doing their job properly. In the nature of cursers he did not have a large vocabulary, just a set of short, sharp, crude expletives, which he used repeatedly *ad nauseam*. He sat in his over-large overcoat, his big hat down over his eyes, wedged into a crack of rock in a high pinnacle of the granite hills, and stared out over the whitened plain. 'Waal, God damn him, here he comes,' he said as he saw the Texan heading towards him, looking more like a ghost than ever on his grey, his coat and face matted by a fresh shower of snow. 'He's gonna go through the pass. He's mine. I've got him. Come on, you lousy Texan bastard, like a lamb to the slaughter. Your fancy pistols won't save you this time. I'm ready for yer.'

He scrambled down from his perch and climbed on to the strong-shouldered paint, riding along the cliff top, making sure to keep off the rim and out of sight, until he reached a spot he had already reconnoitred. Perfect! He climbed down through the rubble of rocks until he found a spur of cliff, like a theatre box from which he had a fine view of the narrow pass below, and of any rider going along it. He lay down, easing a slug into the breech of his carbine. He gripped the butt steady, peered along the sights and waited ...

Black Pete's thoughts had drifted back to the princess, and Frog, and Red Bone and the reward money. The $2,000. That was a hell of a lot. Man could build a real fancy ranch house, have enough for a year's wages for his hired hands. Maybe he would go back to Texas, after all, raise a herd. There were thousands of wild longhorns wandering loose in the brush just waiting to be rounded up and taken to market, so he'd heard. And it was a darn sight warmer than these parts. He would take Spotted Frog. Maybe she and his Spanish gal would get along. He could have two wives. If those Mormons up in Salt Lake City did, why shouldn't he? How many was it their old leader had, forty-five?

He knew it was a crazy idea but a man's head filled with all sort of crazy ideas when he was wandering out in the wilderness day after day. He began to croon a saucy saloon song about Brigham Young sitting in his big bed with all his wives in their little beds on either side.

He made a kissing sound and eased the horse up a steep shale ascent to reach the opening of the narrow defile which would take him across the ridge of hills. The mare paused at the top, twitched her ears and whinnied.

'Whasser matter?' She probably remembered the herd of wild pigs they had come face to face with the last time they had ventured up such a narrow chasm. It had been a hairy moment. 'Or is it my singing you don't like? C'mon.' He gave her a touch of his spurs and she bounded on along the pass. 'Where was I? How does the next verse go?'

Jake peered over the edge and saw the Texan coming. He was making a terrible belly-aching noise. What was wrong with him? When he got nearer he saw he was singing, or trying to. Sounded more like a bear with a sore head. Jake had prepared one of his gunpowder bombs in a leather pouch to throw down at him. The Texan hadn't got a snowball's chance in hell. That's if Jake didn't get him with his first shot. He squinted along the sights and his hairy face split into a grin of revenge.

'"Not you, my dear, Brig Young replied",' Pete sang. '"It's time for number forty-five. Makes me feel good to be alive. So up jumps a gal of sweet sixteen"—' He glanced up and caught sight of a glimmer of sun on steel and hauled his bronc over with all his might as the explosion barrelled along the walls of the pass and a bullet chipped rock near where he had just been. It went whining and ricocheting away.

'Sweet Jesus!' He fumbled to pull his rifle out of the saddle boot, blowing on his frozen fingers, pulling off his glove with his teeth to give his trigger finger more freedom. He jumped from the horse, gave it a slap and sent it cantering back down the pass. He leapt across to a rock on the other side, ducked down as another bullet whined past his ear.

Jake had knelt up, straining to see where he was. Before he could duck back down Pete had fired the Winchester. The slug made Jake tumble backwards with fright. He dropped his bomb with its burning fuse which he had been just about to toss over the edge. 'Aw, shee-it!' The bomb had rolled away. He scrambled to retrieve it. The fuse fizzled merrily. 'Aw, no!' Jake's boots slipped on the icy rock and he fell spreadeagled over it. They were the last words he spoke.

Down in the pass Pete heard a terrific booming sound up above. He dived for cover back to the other side and felt the earth shake as a shower of rocks and itty-bitty bloody pieces of Mad Jake came tumbling and bouncing down.

When the landfall finally ceased and the dust cleared Pete stood and gave a low whistle as one of his dollars came drifting down. He put out a hand and caught it. 'Waal, whadda ya know? Looks like that's all the change he's left me.'

He scratched the back of his head and looked at the pile of rubble blocking the pass. 'Looks like we're gonna have to find another way round. He's sure done a fancy job of burying himself.'

As he climbed back down the pass to look for his horse he muttered, 'That feller allus was a durn nuisance. Good riddance to him.'

Spotted Frog rode out of Fort Sill on her pony soon after they had brought in the princess. Sophie had offered her a silver dollar for her trouble. The Indian girl looked at it and tossed it away, disdainfully. She hated her. She wished she had killed her. She knew the Texan preferred his own kind of woman. It was only natural, she supposed. Two troopers tried to coax her into a stable, but she knew what they wanted. She jumped on to her mount and hurried away from that place. She knew they would not stop pestering her. When she was young, it was true, she had gone with them willingly for the baubles, the bells and coloured ostrich feathers they proffered, cheap gimcracks she could have bought from any trader. Those men were nothing to her. And when her family threw her out she had to go with them as a matter of survival. The Texan was the first white man who had been kind to her, had stepped in and defended her. He was truly a great warrior, fierce and strong, but also gentle. She had hoped he would take her as his squaw, but she was not sure he really wanted her.

She rode for several days through the snow, cutting a shelter of pine boughs at night in the depths of the woods, huddled in her blanket by a small fire, listening to the shrill cries of the night-prowling animals. She thought of the Texan and it kept her strong. He was afraid of no man, no animal. But would he have been strong enough to fight the fierce Comanche single-handed?

When she reached Frenchman's Lake

she washed her body in the icy water. She wanted to pray and purify herself before returning to her people. She looked at her dark-skinned body pitted with tattoos. Some white men laughed when they saw her breasts. To a Wichita tribal tattoos were things of beauty. It was true. They were different humans. They just did not think in the same way. The Wichita were a highly religious, civilized and industrious tribe. They were adept at weaving and pottery, grew crops of corn, beans, tobacco and melons and travelled in the summer hunting buffalo. In the winter they built large communal houses of tree boughs, thatched with grass, where they lived in peaceful harmony using their stores of food until the snows had gone. They had their own legends, their own history passed on through the generations. As she rode north along the shore of the lake, Spotted Frog began to feel glad, and her heart leapt when she saw a cluster of hive-shaped homes of her people.

First, though, she had to face the hostile questions of her father, mother and family. They stood at the door of their house stony-faced as the tribe watched. She told them of her grandfather's death and his last words that they allow her back. 'You sent me away into exile because I disgraced you. I am not bad any more. I have found a good man. A white man.'

'A white man!' Her father wore his hair long for he was a *shaman* like his father before him. The other men had their skulls close-shaven with only a scalplock protruding. In former days it would have been a challenge: try to take my scalp! Now, however, they lived in peace, but they still tattooed their bodies, shaved their heads. 'You still disgrace us!'

'He will come here. He wants to take me as his squaw.'

'If you marry this man you will be cast out forever. We want no white man in our tribe.'

'Who else will marry me?' she asked, as

tears welled into her eyes. 'None of the men here will.'

'I will marry you.' A young warrior stepped forward, a boy who had been her childhood friend. He turned to face the others. 'I know Spotted Frog is a good and true Wichita girl. I would like to take her as my wife.'

'I do not know,' the girl murmured. 'The Texan—'

'You had better come inside,' her father said.

The pass was blocked with rubble but Pete had managed to haul the grey by her reins to scramble over it. He had taken a look around, but all that was left was a bit of Mad Jake's hat. His cash and gold dust, if he had it, had been blown to smithereens. He did, however, find his paint horse and was glad to have her back. He looked at the spur marks on her sides and clucked his tongue. 'Treat you bad, did he, gal? Doncha worry none. That nasty ole man's gone—gone to Hell.'

He was riding past the southern tip of Frenchman's Lake when he saw a mass of blue-coated cavalry approaching. It was too late to take cover, so he stood his ground. At the head of the troops was none other than the long-haired dandy, Custer, himself. 'Howdy,' Pete said, giving a curt salute.

'What's this we've found?' Custer smiled as his men laughed. 'A grey-coat Johnny Reb.'

'I ain't Reb no more,' Pete drawled. 'Jest happens to be the only coat I got.'

'Get off that horse. Search him, Sergeant.'

A corporal covered the Texan with his revolver as a burly sergeant went through his pockets and hollered, 'Lookee here, General.' He brandished the ruby necklace, bracelet and the ring. 'Who's he stole these from?'

'They belong to Princess Sophie. She's offered me a reward if I take them back.'

'Yeah, that's what they all say.' The sergeant cuffed him with his fist across his chin. 'Who you git 'em from, I asked?'

'That's enough, Sergeant,' Custer snapped out. 'You, my fine fellow, must be this wild Texan, this bounty hunter the princess spoke of.'

'That's me, Pete Bowen. I've killed Red Bone, if it's him you're out looking for. You can save yourself the bother. His people will be well away across the plain by now.'

'Don't tell me my business, Texan. We are out hunting hostiles and hostiles we will hunt.' He studied a piece of paper handed up to him. 'Took the oath in Nevada, did you?'

'That's right. I'm a free citizen of the United Stated going about my business. And those three fellas who killed the Russkies' servants they're all dead, too. I took care of the last one myself Or should I say he took care of himself. Got kinda careless with his gunpowder. You'll find his memorial blocking the pass.'

'This seems to be in order.' Custer let the oath of allegiance certificate flutter away on the breeze. 'I suppose we have to let you go. On your way, Texan. You'll find the princess and her brother at the fort. Just behave yourself.'

'The Indians round here don't want war. You'll do no good, Custer, stirring up trouble.'

'Forward, men.' Custer ignored him and spurred his horse forward. Dandy he might be, but he had earned the name Hard Ass for the hours he spent in the saddle. 'We have Comanches to catch,' he cried.

'Damn murdering Yankee,' Pete said, chasing after his dog-eared certificate and watching them go west. 'Waal, I guess I might as well go see Spotted Frog 'fore I go into Fort Sill.' He climbed back on the grey and, leading the paint, headed north along the lake shore.

'What's the matter with that young fella?'

Pete was sitting cross-legged in one of the warm beehive huts chewing on the guts of some cooked animal. A titbit no doubt reserved for visiting white men. 'Why's he keep staring at me like that?'

'He wants to marry me,' the girl said. 'He is challenging you to fight for me.'

'That why he's got a grip on his tommy-hawk like that? After my scalp, eh? Waal, I told you you'd find a real admirer one of these days, gal.' Pete tried to swallow the guts down. What with smoking her father's peace pipe he felt kinda queasy. 'I sure ain't got no wish to fight with him.'

Spotted Frog spoke to the young warrior, who spat out words at Pete. 'I tell him you will not fight him and he say you a coward. I say this is not true.'

The Texan chuckled into his beard. 'Sure got yourself a real banty rooster there, gal. Do you want to marry him?'

'Do *you* want to marry me?' she asked.

'Waal, if you were promised to this boy, mebbe it's best you go back to him.

Because me, I been promised for a long time to a gal down south. And mebbe I'd better go back look for her. It's good your father and his tribe will have you back, Spotted. You can be a good Wichita. And me, I guess it's best I rejoin my tribe.'

The girl smiled through her tears at him. 'You are a good and wise man, Black Pit, for a white man.' She translated what he had said and the boy's face lit up with a smile. He must have heard of the white man's fighting prowess. 'My father says you are welcome to stay here the night. He thanks you.'

'Nope, I'd better be moseyin' on.'

The Texan got to his feet, said his goodbyes and went out to his horses. Spotted Frog followed him out. 'You folks sure know how to make yourselves comfortable,' he said, glancing around the village. 'You belong here, Frog. You're home now.'

He took her hand and pressed it gently for a while, looking into her eyes. 'We had fun, didn't we? But you gotta be a good gal now.' He swung into the saddle and called out, 'Take care. You got yourself a fine brave.'

He cantered out of the village and when he turned to look back Spotted Frog was standing amid her family. The young warrior had his arm around her shoulders. Pete gave a wave and cantered on.

Seventeen

The parade ground of Fort Sill and its surrounding cabins, barracks and stables in their stockade was practically deserted when the Texan rode in. If he was going on down to Texas he would be needing some vittles so he sought out the sutler's store.

'What you want here, stranger?' the bald-headed sutler asked, eyeing Pete's grey frockcoat. 'Ain't still fightin' the war, are ya?'

'No. I got business with them two Russian hunters.'

'The Russkies? They gawn.'

'Gone? The princess and her brother, the count?'

'Princess? Count? Is that what you call 'em? Heck!' The sutler gave a snort of contempt. 'You better join the queue.

Everybody's lookin' fer them two.'

'What do you mean gone? Where they gone to?'

'Waal, they was asking me details of the stage to Kansas City. That was six days ago. I thought it was odd myself as I understood she was gonna go wed that Captain Hazeltin down in Too-sohn. But she said she had to go buy her trousseau. Saw 'em git on the stage the next marnin'.'

'Kansas City? When you reckon the princess is likely to be back? I got business with her, I tell ya?'

'Yeah, so have a lot of other folks, including me. When I went into Fort Gibson to cash that li'l bastard's cheque they laughed in my face. They been droppin' cheques all the way back to the Big River.'

'So where you reckon they gone?'

'Chicago, mebbe. And points east hot foot. I reckon we seen the last of them two. Not only do they owe me near on a thousand dollars for all the damn horses, food and wine, guns and bullets they had, they had the nerve to offload their pelts and huntin' trophies on me. I paid in good gold.'

'Hang on, you tellin' me this count and this princess—'

'Bless you, man, they ain't no more a count and princess than you and me. Nor Russkies, neither.'

'What?' Pete's voice had gone hoarse with shock and anger. 'But she owes me two thousand dollars reward for recovering her property.' He banged the ruby necklace on the counter. 'I near lost my scalp for this.'

The sutler shrugged. 'They owe a lot of people. Rumour is she stung ole Hard Ass himself for three thousand dollars. He's gonna be kicking hisself. Libby'll give him hell. I did hear it whispered that li'l charmer squirmed another thousand out of General Sheridan but I wouldn't go repeating that.'

'Jeez!' Pete gave a whistle of awe. 'You don't say? So why don't them bigwigs get 'em arrested?'

'Because they ain't willing to admit they been made fools of.'

'But if they ain't Russkies how come they had them Russkie servants? That Marie, an' the others that are dead?'

'A family of Russian immigrants down on their luck they picked up. Them two big un's were persuaded to act like Cossack guards. It was one big hoax, I tell ya. They've taken everybody in, all the way along the line from Fort Smith. Everybody thought they was millionaires and gave as much credit as they wanted. Including me. We all bin gypped.'

'Waal, I'll be a blue-assed baboon.' Pete's face split into a grin of awe. 'You sayin they're a coupla con artists?'

'The best. They got a record a mile long. They ain't even brother and sister. It came through on the wire this mornin' from Fort Gibson to have 'em arrested, but the birds have flown the coop.'

'Where'n hell they from, then?'

'New Orleans, last I heard. They got thrown off the riverboats for doing a double-sharp at cards. She was giving him the signals, you know? And from there they came on out here. He's an outawork actor. She started off in a New Orleans cathouse. I bet they're laughing their socks off.'

'Waal, I dunno. I guess you gotta see the funny side. But I been robbed of three thousand I was planning to put down on a ranch, so I was hoping the princess would come up with two thousand. I sure have been had.'

'You could allus apply for town dog-catcher.'

'Very funny.' Pete fumbled in his pocket for the ten-dollar bills rescued from the Comanche fire. 'At least these should cover some flour and, less see, a jug of whiskey is what I need.'

The sutler looked at them, screwed them up and tossed them over his shoulder.

'Forgeries. That came over the wire, too. I got plenty of them in my drawer.'

'No! You don't say? I thought it odd they'd got the president's head on 'em so soon.' He put the ring and bracelet alongside the necklace. 'I figure I'm entitled to keep these. How much will ya give me?'

The sutler picked them up and held them against the light. 'A glass of water.'

'*What?* She said they were priceless.'

'They are. Price-*less*. Fakes. Like all the rest of that jewellery she had. Good imitations, though. Tell you what, stranger, I'll go to ten dollars. Some captain's lady might like 'em.'

'Hell, no. I'll keep 'em, in that case.' He shoved them back into his greatcoat pocket. 'Hang on, here's some silver the count paid out to them guides of his.' He tested the coin with his teeth and felt it give. 'Don't tell me—'

'Theatre money,' the sutler grinned. 'Convincing ain't it? Like that phoney accent of his. Zis and zat. The nearest he's been to Russia is New York.'

'Jeesis, he sure caught me.' He found the green-back that had fluttered from Mad Jake's last resting place and proffered it. 'I've an idea this is one of mine. It's real enough, ain't it?'

The sutler examined it. 'Yeah. Thass OK. That'll buy you a coupla cans of these newfangled tins of peaches. You should try 'em. Better than the real thing. Amazing what they come up with these days.'

'Really? Good. We're in business.' When the sutler had opened a can for him he fished a half peach out. 'Mm. Real tasty. How much I got left? Enough for some flour?'

He made his purchases and strolled to the door. 'It's been an interestin' experience, but I cain't wait to git back to Texas.'

'So long, stranger.'

'So long.'

He forded the Red River at Doan's Crossing and put the horses' tails to the wind, ambling on his way, day after day, eating up the miles, one rolling rise after another until the snow had gone and the air was warmer.

When he reached San Antonio he had a meal in the Spanish town, good southern food, tacos spiced with hot chilli, washed down with a beer. He still had the gold coins sewn in his belt. They would give him a start. He spent the night in a stable with his horses.

In the morning he went at a brisk trot out towards the horse ranch run by Louisa's father. He wasn't sure what he would find. Not even sure that they were still there, it had been so long, but his hopes were high. Half a mile from the ranch house Pete hauled in and grinned to himself. He pulled the bullet-scarred Rebel flag from his pack, the St Andrew's cross on blood red, the stars of the thirteen secessionist states, and stuck it on the Comanche lance he had brought along as a souvenir. He kicked the horses into a gallop and giving the wild, keening Johnnie Reb yell that had scared the daylights out of many a blue-belly he went charging towards the house and corrals. His heart missed a beat when he saw a slim, dark-haired girl run out on to the porch.

'Pete!' Her voice was tremulous as she stared at the dark-bearded rider in his frock coat and *chaparejos* who swirled his horses to a halt in front of her. 'Is that you?'

'Sure is, Honey. I ain' no ghost. I made it through. I'm still in one piece an' lucky to be 'live.'

'But it's been five years. I—'

'Got held up. You ain't wed yet?'

'No, But—'

'You dang sure will be.' He pulled the ruby necklace, and bracelet from his pocket, threw them to her. 'Here's your weddin' present for the time bein'.' He beckoned her over, reached down for her hand and slipped the ring on her finger. 'Here's your engagement ring. I gotta tell ya, it ain't real and it's second-hand.'

'It's beautiful,' she said, staring at it on her hand.

'*Quien es?*' A grey-haired man in a sombrero and leathers rode up, a rifle in his hand. 'Ees that you, Pete?'

'Sure is.' He swung down and put an arm around Louisa. 'Me an' your gal gotta lotta catchin' up to do.'

'See!' The Mexican grinned. 'I told you he would be back.'

The publishers hope that this book has given you enjoyable reading. Large Print Books are especially designed to be as easy to see and hold as possible. If you wish a complete list of our books, please ask at your local library or write directly to: Dales Large Print Books, Long Preston, North Yorkshire, BD23 4ND, England.

This Large Print Book for the Partially sighted, who cannot read normal print, is published under the auspices of

THE ULVERSCROFT FOUNDATION